Sergeant Delancy handed Madden a business card. "Get some sleep, Joe. Then give me a call some-time tomorrow. And no more crazy stunts like tonight."

When the door was closed, Madden leaned back against it. As he heard the big cop's footfalls move down the hall toward the elevator, he grinned. The stitches hurt even through the dullness of the novocaine, but the hurt felt right somehow. He had to get himself together, both physically and mentally. Because he had a plan.

It wasn't much of a plan, not yet. But he had the outline for what he was going to do. *You're sup-posed to be the engineer,* Delancy had said. It was obvious to Madden, even in his present state, that some engineering in this city was badly needed. But the big cop was dead right about the rest, too.

No more crazy stunts like tonight.

No. The nights to come were going to be a lot different.

*A hell of a lot different!*

## The Vigilante Series

# The Vigilante

## New York:

## AN EYE FOR AN EYE

### by V.J. Santiago

PINNACLE BOOKS • NEW YORK CITY

VIGILANTE: (NEW YORK) AN EYE FOR AN EYE

Copyright © 1975 by Lyle Kenyon Engel

An original Pinnacle Books edition, published for the first time anywhere.

ISBN: 0-523-00714-0

First printing, November 1975

Printed in the United States of America

PINNACLE BOOKS, INC.
275 Madison Avenue
New York, N.Y. 10016

# AN EYE FOR AN EYE

# PROLOGUE

New York. It is four o'clock on a February morning. It has been officially Monday for three hours, and it is quiet on East Seventy-seventh Street, at least on that portion of it between First and Second Avenues.

Her name is Janet. She is twenty-two and from a small town in Nebraska. She is doing well at the trade she is learning in the city, that of an advertising copy writer. She has short cropped brown hair. She is attractive, both of face and slim figure. She wears a long red and white striped nightshirt which is too big for her but is comfortable. Covering her in the bed are a sheet and two blankets.

She is asleep. Or she has been. Just now, she suddenly is awake, wide awake, and she doesn't know why. An ice cold chill of fear runs the full length of her spine. Again, she doesn't know why.

There is no sound reaching her ears, nothing. There is no movement within the range of her open eyes, no change in the position of anything within the range of the small electric clock light which casts a pale orange light from the side of the bed she is facing. And yet—

She is afraid—deathly afraid.

So much so that she dare not turn, dare not look to

the foot of the bed or to its other side. She is afraid that she might see something, some—one.

And then she hears it. From behind and above her. The heavy breathing which comes after someone has held his breath—and the voice:

"Scream and you're dead. Turn around."

*Oh, my God, please no . . .*

"I said turn around. Look at me."

Trembling with the fright which has gripped her stomach and heart with frozen fingers, she jerks her head around. She sees the dark shadowed form, dimly lighted by orange. She looks only fleetingly at the eyes and face she cannot make out. It is the long pointed knife, gleaming with brightness, which captures her focus.

"H-How—"

But she doesn't continue. How did you get in? That was the question she had in mind, but that's not important now. Why. That's the real point now.

And deep within her, she knows why.

"I've watched you, Janet, watched you very carefully. I hope you don't try to scream. I'll have to kill you then, and you wouldn't want that, would you?" The voice is young sounding, almost pleasant, but then it turns less pleasant. *"Would you?"*

"N-No. Please—"

"Just remember, Janet. No screaming. My knife will be in my hand the whole time . . ."

He reaches toward her, bending over, placing one knee on the bed. *God . . .* If only she could blank out, if only she might not *feel* what was coming . . .

And then his fingers touch her neck, and despite herself, the top half of her body lurches upward, her mouth opens, and—

She feels the sharp steel enter her side, even with her left breast. "You—"

*You're not human!* The thought flashes through her brain, but she can't vocalize it as the knife blade is removed and she falls back to the pillows. She feels the sudden rush of cold air on her flesh as the covers and sheet are torn from her, as the long nightshirt is ripped upward. And then she feels the pressure on the bed between her thighs. "N-Nnnn—"

"I'm sorry, Janet. But you broke the rules, you see."

*I—I broke the rules? The rules? Good God, I—*

But she can't say her thoughts, because his hand is clamped tightly over her mouth. And as he lowers himself upon her, she feels his thrusting, painful entry.

*Oh my God my God my God my—*

And then suddenly it is over. He lifts his weight from her. She thinks he must be smiling now, but she dare not open her eyes to see the face above her. But his voice is soft again.

"Thank you, Janet. You were one of the best."

There is something in his words which strike her with rage—or outrage—and she pushes herself upward from the mattress. For a brief moment she thinks her move was a mistake, that she might have provoked him, but no—

The gleaming knife already had begun its movement before she had begun hers.

She feels only the very beginning of the point striking home just above her heart.

Twenty minutes after four in the morning, a lone man steps from an apartment building and onto the sidewalk facing Seventy-seventh Street. The street is quiet, and as he heads east, only his own footfalls reach his ears. In

3

the buildings around him no one suspects that a murder has been committed so very nearby. Most people will never know it. Those who find out will have to wait until two days pass, when Janet's body is discovered.

Joe Madden will not be one of those to know. Because, before this Monday in February is over, Joe Madden—whose apartment building is directly across the street from the dead Janet's—will be absorbed in the death of someone even closer to him.

There will be no connection between the two deaths.

There will be every possible connection between the two deaths.

Both truths are of the kind which have to be learned.

At twenty minutes after four o'clock in this February Monday morning, Joe Madden has somewhat less than twenty hours to learn those truths.

This Monday, for Joe Madden, is going to be a deadly day.

4

# ONE

It was going to be one of those days—one of the kind that comes but rarely, and that at least was a damned good thing.

Joe Madden knew it right from the moment his eyelids snapped open and he turned to face the battery-operated digital alarm clock to the right side of the bed. The large letters and numbers proclaimed their message slightly out of focus, but clear enough.

He sat up sharply, then leaned his naked back against the pillows. With his right index finger he reached over and gently prodded the nude shoulder of the woman who shared his bed, the woman whose immediate response was to abruptly turn her back to him and pull the sheet and covers snugly under her chin. His shoulder-target having shifted, he gripped a handful of her long blonde hair and tugged at it lightly.

"Go-way," came a sleepy voice.

"I plan to," he replied. "But there's something you ought to know."

"I know. You love me."

"That's true."

"I love you too. Now let me sleep." The voice had lost none of its drowsiness.

5

"Sara, there's something else you ought to know. Something you ought to see."

"Can't," she murmured. "My eyes are closed."

He reached back to the table for the clock, then placed it directly in front of her closed eyes. "Open them—just for a moment."

"Can't. Not till morning."

He held the clock stationary with his left hand. With his right, he formed an index finger-thumb pincer and burrowed under the covers until he made contact with target.

"Ouch!" Sara cried out. Then her eyes caught the letters and numbers before her.

*MON 9:15*

"Ouch!" she repeated. She sat up straight in the bed, the falling covers revealing a delicate but very shapely top half of a nude body. Before Joe Madden had a chance to appreciate the scene, however, she was up and out of the bed and padding from the room—revealing, although fleetingly, her just-as-shapely and just-as-nude bottom half. As he climbed from the covers and made his way toward the bathroom, he heard the start of the bubbling sound of the coffee perculator.

"No time for that!" he called out to the kitchen. "A shave and shower and that's all." But even as he put toothbrush to toothpaste and began the scrubbing motion to fight potential dentist bills, he knew that he'd make time to have at least a sip of the coffee. *MON 9:15*—as bad as it had begun—could at least support a sip of coffee, right?

It was his fault, and he knew it. In the three months he and Sara had been married, they had each sort of fallen into certain responsibilities which the other counted upon. Such as Sara's readying the coffee pot each

6

night before they went to bed. Such as his setting the alarm. Last night, however . . .

He found his own eyes in the large mirror over the sink, reaching for the hot water faucet with his left hand and the aerosol shaving cream can with his right. *You're a lucky man, Joe Madden,* his mirror image told him. *Lucky as hell.*

In the last three months it had amounted to what had become an every-morning ritual. This morning, with both of them already fifteen, probably twenty minutes late for work, the ritual would have to be dispensed with—except that it wasn't.

It was not that Joe Madden was vain, that wasn't it at all. Even though at forty-three he had quite a bit, he thought, to be vain about. His six-foot frame was not overly muscled, but he didn't look all that bad now, naked as the proverbial jaybird. No extra paunch—well, there was the start of one, yes, but once the warm weather came and they could get out of Manhattan on weekends more often, to the beach, that would disappear, he vowed it so—and the face, that looked healthy, too.

Not really a handsome face, not by filmstar definitions, no. It looked too hard in places, around the eyes and cheekbones—and the chin was just a bit too jutting. The eyes were a soft blue, which might have been all right if his complexion had been lighter, but his skin color was that of a man who seemed to have a perpetual suntan. There was French-Canadian (and somewhere back there probably Indian) blood that accounted for that, as well as for the straight jet-black hair which, although it betrayed not even a single evidence of gray, wasn't all that manageable at the hair lengths fashionable to the male of the human species these days. Thus

7

his hair wasn't as long as Sara would have liked it, but its thick and unruly shocks fell slightly over the tops of his ears and down a bit past his collar to the rear and down almost to his thick black eyebrows to the front.

He was not quite "in" but, as he'd made it plain to Sara, "I'm an engineer, not a guitar-slapping hippie. I've got to travel all over the place—to places where what's *in* in New York looks downright disgusting to local eyes. And I'm not in a position to educate the heathen."

"You look lovely," was her standard response.

It was a response that he himself had grown to love. If there ever came a day when she stopped responding like that . . .

He laughed. No, that was unthinkable. Sara and he . . .

She was—everything. Twenty-nine, beautiful, talented—she earned a good twenty-three thousand additional dollars, she being a fashion designer, and as far as his cold engineering eyes could tell, a damned good one—but more than all that, she was what he needed. Sara was his second wife, the first marriage having ended—for him—in the dusty forlorn town of Juarez. That was in 1967, seemingly an age ago. He would have completely forgotten Helen had it not been for the alimony checks of the following three years. Then, when he praised the Powers for her remarriage, the necessity of paying over a good percentage of his ample salary vanished, and he recognized then—and perhaps only then—that it hadn't really been Helen's fault. The chemistry just hadn't been there.

Fortunately there had been no children. If there had been, things might have worked out differently, but he didn't really think so. They had married too young, set their sights on the wrong goals of life—most of them to

8

do with status such as the too-large house in Baldwin, Long Island—and worked hard at everything except what really counted: the sharing of a marriage. Even had they worked at it, he wasn't all that certain that they could have made it good. Chemistry, maybe. It must have been there at the beginning, although he wasn't even sure of that. What did either of them know of *real* chemistry when they made that foolish trip to the altar?

The second time, though, *his* second time, it was all different. Sara and he had known each other for a little more than a year, and the decision to marry had not been made lightly by either of them. But it was a right decision, he knew it. What's more, every day at least once, she did the kind of thing which made him certain that *she* knew it as well.

He had half of his face shaved when she appeared in the mirror beside him. She still was totally nude, her fine-boned delicate face looking a little disappointed.

"The coffee's terrible. I think I didn't put enough in the pot."

He gulped the grapefruit juice from the glass she'd put on the counter. "I should have waited until *after* you'd completed all your chores last night. Sexual heat fouls up your other functions." He was referring to the fact that it was Sara's routine to load the morning coffee pot the night before.

"Other people, too—like those who are supposed to set morning alarms." She made a playful grab for him in the nether region.

"Hey. I'll cut myself! Besides, you had your orgy last night—almost all night." But the old familiar feeling was stirring in his loins, and visually so.

"Joe, I've got an idea . . ." The way she trailed off the

word, the way her eyes met his in the mirror, left little for the imagination concerning just what that idea might be.

"Sorry. Client in from L.A. today. They're probably stalling the hell out of him right now."

She loaded up her toothbrush. "Important client?"

He slapped her backside with the excess shaving cream he'd taken from his face. "Sara, my dear, there is no such thing as an *un*important client."

"Okay. You might be sorry, though. I just might have an affair with some handsome man this afternoon."

"Uh-uh. Wait until after work. I'll meet you for a drink, then dinner, and then back home. We'll keep our affair right in the family."

"Uh-uh yourself. Not tonight."

"You planning on having a headache or something?"

"Something." She looked genuinely sorry. "You'll probably have the headache. We're dining with Jean and Dan tonight, remember?"

He remembered. Scowling, he also remembered his first impression of the morning. It very definitely had the makings of being a very bad day.

Out in the cold gray February morning version of East Seventy-seventh Street, he walked west in the rapid pace that is what New Yorkers term walking. His watch said nine forty-five. Decision time. Go up to Lexington and hit the subway or try to pick up a cab on Second? No decision necessary—or no trying. At the corner of Seventy-seventh and Second, the cab was there. He flagged it automatically. The expense was justified under the circumstances, and the more leisurely ride downtown would give him more time to collect his thoughts about the conference which, he was sure, would take up most of the day, lunch included.

The offices of Chilton and Harris were located in Rockefeller Center. A prestigious location for a prestigious firm. Under the bronze nameplate just outside the elevator were the words *Consulting Engineers* plus an arrow directing the visitor to the left where he would find at a large reception desk an even larger woman in her fifties. Formidable as was the harpylike widowed Mrs. Greene (there was the office rumor that she ate her husband alive), she had, under that snarling all-business exterior, a heart of gold. Or so the older members of the firm claimed. Joe Madden, four years with the company, was a relative newcomer and had not experienced a single instance of Mrs. Greene's warmer side.

"You're late," was her greeting as he approached her desk. He waited for the rest. There would be more, he was certain, for her right hand had not yet produced the key to his office. It took two keys to unlock the door, one of which was on a chain in his pocket, the other always returned to the custody of Mrs. Greene. There were no master keys. Should a loss of either take place, a locksmith would have to be called. Madden always had thought this stress on security was just a little much. He also suspected that there was a bit of showmanship involved, since the building was duly protected by an amply manned security service. But the old-timers insisted it was no game. "We've got some unpatented stuff we play around with, Joe, stuff that might be worth a lot of money to somebody other than our clients."

In any case, the double-lock system was in force. Thus Madden now waited for Mrs. Greene to stop snarling and hand him his key. After she had her further say, of course. She did not look at him but down into the middle drawer of her desk.

"Mr. Crosby has been worried. He's been expecting you."

"Fine. His desire will be fulfilled in triplicate, since I am now here."

Still no key, still her eyes focused within the drawer.

"Had me call your apartment, he did. I called several times. There was no answer. I suppose you and the wife weren't home."

"That's right," Madden said. "Sunday nights we always spend with our respective lovers."

Greene's head snapped up. It did Madden good to see her open mouth. He held out his hand, trying to look serious as she dumbly dropped the key into his palm. He started to turn down the hall, then paused. Her eyes were still on him, her mouth was open. Should he? Yes.

"That's the problem with taking lovers, Mrs. Greene. It really is. They keep you awake at night. My friend—well, I want to tell you—he snored the whole night long."

"H—*He*?" She almost gagged on the word.

Madden winked. "Fred," he said confidentially. "My wife's hairdresser."

The secretary he and Hal Crosby shared sighed with relief. "He has Mr. Grossman in there with him." She turned toward the closed door to Crosby's office, then back to Madden. "I've been inside with coffee twice, and the mood was not all that cordial. I think, Mr. Madden, that you're expected."

He handed his briefcase and the two keys to the girl—Jill Stanly, her name was. "Okay. I'll go in now.

On the top right-hand corner of my desk there's a manila folder—no, wait. There is a pile of folders. The one I want is"—he thought about it only for a second; his almost totally reliable, photographic memory was not only the talk of the firm but also had been responsible for his whizz-kid performance in college and graduate school—"third from the top. You'll recognize it from the odd-looking phallic symbol on the cover."

*"Phallic—"*

"You know what that is, Jill?"

Her face was red, but her features firm. "Naturally, I know what that—"

"Naturally."

She sputtered. "What I meant was, I know because I've studied a good deal of literature—"

"I'm sure you have," Madden cut her off. "Now, if you'll hurry along, I'll just—"

*"Mr. Madden!"*

He had turned toward Crosby's door, but now he turned back.

"Mr. Madden. If I might be so bold to ask, why have you taken to drawing phallic symbols on our manila folders?"

He noted with amusement the use of the possessive *our*. They're the firm's folders, buddy, so why are you defacing them with obscenities? He considered telling her the truth: that actually he was doodling while on the phone, that actually the drawing was supposed to represent a dowsing rod—one of those things used by those folks able to use them to locate water and other valuable material—but if he said that he knew he'd appear even more odd than he did now. Who but an odd engineering egghead would try, while carrying on a supposedly serious telephone conversation with an im-

13

portant (they all were, remember that) client, decide out of the blue that there had to be an engineering-scientific reason why those dowsing rods worked?

No, that wouldn't do.

"Why?" he repeated. "Miss Stanly, it's simple enough. I've never learned how to draw vaginas."

He didn't wait for a reaction, but opened Crosby's door.

Hal Crosby shot to his feet. So great and so obvious was his relief that Madden likened the thin bald man's reaction to something he'd expect a woman to have, post-delivery.

Madden smiled at Crosby, then extended his hand to the client.

"Mr. Grossman. How good to see you again."

Grossman lived up to his name. He was a round man with a round red face. His face now was frowning.

"We never met. You maybe met my brother, Herman. I'm Sidney. It's strange you'd mix us up like that, Mr. Madden—at least, I hope, after all this time that you *are* Mr. Madden."

"I am," Madden admitted.

"He is," Crosby confirmed. "He really is."

"Good," Sidney Grossman said. His eyes narrowed as they turned back on Madden. "Funny you'd mix us up, Herman and me. He's fat."

Madden fell into one of the chairs before Crosby's desk with resignation. Christ. It really *was* going to be one of those days. A really deadly one.

Madden, at that moment—twelve minutes after ten in the morning—had absolutely no idea of just how deadly his clock was running.

There was something more than thirteen hours ahead.

14

# TWO

"Please, Joe. I want to celebrate!"

Sara's voice over the telephone was excited. She had a right to be excited. A promotion, hitting her right between her well-deserved eyes. But no, it was impossible, the thing she asked.

"I'd like to have lunch with you, Sara, but—"

"But, hell. Tell them to go and—"

"Believe me, I'd like to. Especially one Mr. Sidney Grossman. But no dice. We'll celebrate tonight. I promise."

"*After* Brooklyn?"

He cursed softly. Jean and Dan. "After and before. A quick drink before we climb on the subway. Name your place."

She did. Ratazzi's. "I love you, Joe," she added.

"You'd goddamn well better," he said. "I don't care how wealthy you've suddenly become."

He said goodbye and went back into Crosby's office. He'd taken the call at Jill's desk. He no sooner opened the door and he heard Grossman's repeated complaint:

"But it was *your* specifications which said—"

Lunch was a disaster. Not the restaurant. Le Vert Galant, in Madden's estimation and that of a lot of other New Yorkers, was one good French restaurant. But, regardless of the full-glass martinis and the excellent French onion soup and what followed, it was probably the worst lunch Madden could recall for a long, long time. The prime reason was Mr. Sidney Grossman.

"*Yech!* I just know that this onion soup is going to give me heartburn!"

And:

"Let's get back to your lousy specifications!"

"Another martini? Good God, that first one was awful. They don't put enough vermouth in them here."

Crosby almost choked on a crouton. "Enough . . . *vermouth?*"

Grossman nodded sourly. "I should have specified. But what good would that have done me? I ask you, you who know *all* about specifications . . ."

Back in the office it was more of the same. The problem was one of diplomacy more than one of engineering. The engineering on the job had been sound, and both Madden and Crosby knew it—as did their bosses, Chilton and Harris. The Brothers Grossman, more than a year ago, had entered the high-speed specialized printing business. Knowing almost nothing about the business, except for their conviction that it would be extremely profitable, they had hired Chilton and Harris to design "from the ground up" the entire works—facilities, processes, manpower organization, everything. It was exactly the kind of "everything engineering" that the firm was known for, and exactly the kind of work those employed by the firm enjoyed. The job, when it was finished, was good, damned good. Madden didn't get warm feelings in the pit of his gut from anything but a good—and complete—job. There had been nothing that wasn't accounted for.

16

Except that there was, something over which none of the Chilton and Harris team had any control

Namely, the Brothers Grossman themselves.

Their first decision was to reject the locations suggested. There were three of them, all suburban to Los Angeles proper. "We got to be near the action!" Sidney said with finality. Or was it Herman? Madden didn't know. Crosby had most of the client contact on this one, and from the horror it turned into, Madden was quite happy with that fact. Of course, setting up in midtown L.A. presented one or two difficulties with the package Chilton and Harris had prepared.

One, since a new building wasn't in the cards, the new printing establishment would have to do with already built quarters. Thus, the work "flow lines" Madden had created with the finesse of a conductor for a Lincoln Center symphony would have to be altered—"just a bit," said whichever of the Grossmans was doing the talking at the moment. Which brings us to—

Two. The already-built quarters, although in "the exact right spot," were somewhat smaller than anticipated in even the first sketches, let alone the final detailed drawings. Thus things were altered "just a bit more."

These alterations, by the way, were not accomplished through any consultation with the Grossmans' engineering firm. Instead, the brothers obtained free "but completely reliable" advice from the representatives of the manufacturers whose equipment they installed. Which brings us to—

Three. The equipment they installed. They "talked around." They "got a couple of bargains." Nothing to change drastically anything at all, nothing except save some money. "You engineering types," laughed Sidney

17

or Herman. "You think nothing but expensive, but we're businessmen. We got to think of profit!"

All of which brings us to—

Four. Profit. Rather, loss. Not only did the new equipment fail to "mesh" as it should have, but the flow lines which had been changed from those Madden had designed didn't flow all that well. In the less than a year of operation, there had been a number of minor mishaps which were bad enough in terms of ruined jobs which had to be rerun, but there had occurred a rather serious accident where one of the firm's sixteen employees was permanently injured. The lawsuit was still undecided, but there were other problems. One involved the sixteen employees. The original plan called for twenty, but "hell, in the city labor's more expensive. Besides, we don't need all those people. We'll pay overtime!" Another problem involved the quarters themselves. Crosby had tried to point out that the rent would cost much more than actually building the quarters which Chilton and Harris recommended, but to no avail.

And now the Grossmans were unhappy. Understandably, Madden thought. But they shouldn't be unhappy with their engineering consultants. There were memos to the file on every deviation the Grossmans made from the original design plan—well, every deviation the engineering firm knew about. No, professionally, neither he nor Crosby nor the company had any obligation at all to Messrs. Grossman. Nonetheless, they were professionals.

"It's like being a doctor," old man Chilton had said the previous Friday. He'd just read to Madden and Crosby the cable which informed them of Grossman's impending visit. The old man didn't like it any better than his two employees. That was obvious from the

18

resigned sigh with which he'd finished his reading. "Just like a doctor, who when a patient disobeys the strictest of orders, can't say the hell with him—although he'd probably like doing nothing better—we too have to give our Mr. Grossman some of our time and some of our patience."

Crosby, who after all had written all those memos to the file, wasn't very happy about it, but he acquiesced. "At what rate of billing?" he asked.

The old man shook his head. "Tell me what's happened after it's happened. We'll work something out."

"Overhead," Crosby had told Madden as they left the top man's office. "General charges to company overhead. That's where it'll go, I'll give you five bucks to your one."

Madden didn't take the bet. He would have given ten to one odds.

And here he was—and Crosby—both of them listening to dear Mr. Grossman taking their engineering abilities to task and watching him read aloud an endless stream of imperfections "in specifications" from a red flip-over note pad which Madden would have liked nothing more than to shove down the reader's throat. He felt he was a knight in shining armor for resisting the urge when finally, flipping the notebook closed, Grossman stared at them both and then asked the key question:

"Well, what is your company prepared to do to make reparation?"

"Sir?" Crosby asked. The break in his voice made the word one of two syllables.

"I asked you, what are you prepared to do for me? Like I just pointed out, it was your specifications which—"

Madden rose. "Mr. Grossman—"

But Crosby cut him off. "Excuse me, *Doctor* Madden—"

"He's a doctor?" Grossman said with an abashed look on his face. "I was hiring engineers, not—"

"I was referring," Crosby moved in quickly, "to Mr. Madden's level of educational attainment."

Like hell he was, Madden thought with a repressed grin. He was referring to old man Chilton's pep talk. But well done, Crosby, well done. Madden took an obvious look at his watch.

"It's almost four forty-five. I hate to rush off, but I've got an appointment. Mr. Grossman, I trust you'll be able to conclude your business with Mr. Crosby—"

"Today?" Grossman said. "What conclude? What have we concluded here today? I ask you—you tell me, Mr. *Doctor* Madden."

Somehow, Madden mumbled something about his dire need to leave. He was grateful to Crosby for saying all the right things to excuse the absence. Good old Hal. Madden had known him for some time, but he'd never used the adjectives "good old" before his name. But now, yes. He owed Hal Crosby something. The poor guy would be tied up for a least another hour with Grossman—and probably tomorrow too, although Madden would have to suffer that as well. But Hal lived out in New Jersey or somewhere. His wife and kids would have to be waiting for supper until he came home. Christ. It was almost enough for Madden to want to stay and help out.

Almost, but, as the saying goes, not quite. Tomorrow was soon enough to face Mr. Sidney Grossman.

And, as he pressed the elevator button and reflected on that horrible thought, he would have welcomed listening to fat Mr. Grossman on the next day. He would have—"

If he had known the alternative—if he had known just how he would be spending the early hours of the following day.

"I love you," she said.

He touched his martini glass to hers. "Congratulations."

"You don't care that I love you?"

"If I didn't care, would I be here now, wasting my time with you when I could be playing doctor?"

He told her of his day, and she laughed with him. It was symptomatic, that laughing. If, during his earlier days—during his days as Helen's husband or later when he was a bachelor—a Sidney Grossman had abused him professionally as he had been abused this day, he would not have smiled for days. It would have seethed inside him until a boiling point was reached. Then would have come the frantic attempt for sudden release. But now . . .

This girl, this Sara, this wife of his . . . she was so very, very good for him. For him and to him.

"I said congratulations. What are you now—head seamstress?"

She frowned. "Joe, I've tried to tell you what I do—"

"And, as a typical male chauvinist pig, I don't let you. You know why?"

"Okay—why? I've sort of been wondering. I thought maybe your male breadwinner type of ego—"

"Ego hell. It's loins."

She repeated his last word.

He nodded. "Damned right. Loins. There I am, listening to you going on about your career and all, and

21

something happens. Maybe it's the way your voice tinkles."

"Tinkles?"

"Who's telling this? Tinkles. That's what it does. Like church bells."

"I'm not all that religious, and you know it."

"Then you should have your voice changed so that it sounds like something more mundane—like maybe garbage can covers being played like cymbals."

"That's very romantic."

"Speaking of which, let's go home. My loins are acting up again."

"Joe, we can't and you know it. Jean is expecting us."

Madden frowned. "Well, maybe we could call her now—before she goes to too much trouble. Tell her that I've come down with a frustrated loin. She wouldn't want that messing up their apartment, would she?"

"We'll make it an early evening, I promise," Sara said.

As Madden ordered two more drinks, he thought about it. No, it wouldn't be an early evening. It never was on those occasions they went to visit Sara's sister and her husband. Something always happened so that dinner was served hours after it should be, and then it just wasn't polite to eat and run. No, it would be at least eleven by the time they'd extricated themselves from his in-laws' apartment, and probably eleven thirty or later by the time they found themselves in their own bed.

Sara seemed to know what he was thinking. "Joe, please. She's my only sister. It'll be early, I do promise."

"I'll hold you to it."

They left Ratazzi's shortly before six. They didn't have to be in Brooklyn until around seven-thirty, but Sara

22

wanted to hit Brentano's bookstore on Fifth Avenue. There was a recent book on some newly discovered notebooks of Da Vinci that she'd wanted for weeks but had kept postponing the buying of because their apartment seemed to be stacked end to end with books she'd bought and hadn't yet read. "But today I feel I owe myself something," she said. "A congratulatory gift from me to me."

She bought the Da Vinci book and two others, one of which was heralded as a manual to survive in this age of energy crises and other shortages. It was basically a back-to-the-land book which told how to build solar energy units on the roof, how to create better mulch for better vegetables. Its relevance to city living was an absolute zero, but the book was selling well, particularly in New York. Which all went to show something or other, Madden decided. Probably what it showed was that most New Yorkers would rather be somewhere else. With all the "excitement and vitality" of Manhattan, there were decidedly some bad features to the great metropolis.

They saw one of the bad features on their way to the subway.

They were walking along Fiftieth, heading for the entrance to the Seventh Avenue downtown train, when it happened. The girl looked to be about Sara's age. She was tall and lean like a fashion model and her clothes matched her looks. Her facial features might well have been pretty-to-beautiful, but it was difficult to tell. Madden had not especially noticed her until it happened. After it happened, her face was contorted into a shrieking hysteria.

It happened fast.

Neither Madden nor Sara got a good look at the man,

even though the whole thing took place less than twenty feet from them. He was black, that they knew, but that was all. He moved like lightning, seeming to appear from nowhere at the side of the dark-haired girl, using his hands to both shove the girl in one direction and to whip her shoulder bag in the other. She had been holding the bag the way women are advised to—strap over shoulder, hand clutching strap at about breast level— but the clutching hand unclutched when she felt herself falling. By the time she recovered her balance, her bag no longer was on the shoulder. It was moving west at a swift, people-dodging run. Even before the girl's screams began, it was too late.

"The city," Madden said under his breath. "It's a goddamned jungle."

Madden's brother-in-law agreed. "Nothing is safe anymore," Dan said. It was nine thirty. Dinner, as predicted, was late, Jean having miscalculated the time it would take for the roast to get done, and so the pre-dinner drinks had amounted to more rounds than normally would have been the case. Madden nursed the beer before him. Tomorrow was going to be bad enough without his having a hangover to nurse. As for Dan, who did something of a supervisory nature with an insurance company, he didn't slow down at all, both in terms of drinking and talking.

Madden didn't care much for Dan, a thirty-year-old who spent a good deal of his time lifting weights and jogging and whatever other activities the local YMCA offered the sweatsuit set. Aside from an admittedly good physique, the man was a slob in Madden's opinion, both in his manner and in his thinking. What's more, he was an obnoxious slob, rarely missing an occasion to pose with muscles flexed—a lot like the models on the covers of those fag magazines. Madden in fact wondered whether there was a little of the fag in Dan; he did after all seem to go out of his way to act and talk "manly."

But what the hell. Madden didn't have to suffer the man all that much. Only on these rare occasions when dinner was offered, either here or at his and Sara's apartment. And Jean, after all, was Sara's sister. He felt sorry for the woman, some two or three years older than Sara. She had followed Sara from Chicago to New York, hoping to catch some of the glamorous life her sister had written home about. Instead she had caught Dan.

"It *is* a goddamned jungle," Dan said, his tongue a little thick from the Scotch he'd been drinking. "And it's as bad out here as it is in Harlem, almost. It's not safe to walk the streets, not at night anyway." He sneered in Sara's direction. "Where's all those beautiful people of yours when it gets dark? I'll tell you where. They're locked up in their apartments with three or four locks on the door, shaking in their boots every time the building creaks, that's where they are."

Sara tried to smile. She didn't care much for Dan, either. "You may be overstating your point," she said.

"Maybe. But if people had sense, that's where they would be. In the daytime the city might belong to working people like you and me, but at night it belongs to them. And, aside from living on what they can steal, you know who supports them? You know who gives them welfare checks and food stamps and keeps them alive so they can keep on robbing and killing? Me, that's who. Me and you. I'll tell you this, I'm only hanging around here until I can swing a transfer—maybe to Hartford. That would be the thing. But you know what?

They can't get anybody to come to New York. That's a fact. Only the young guys just out of college. Those the company can get to come here because they don't know what it's like here. To get a guy with experience—somebody to replace me—would be like pulling teeth. So here I sit. Well, I'm not going to just stay sitting. I'm gonna tell them, and I mean it. I'm gonna have it out with the big guys. Look here, I'll say . . ."

And he continued saying, to Madden's growing discomfort. Finally the call to the dinner table offered temporary reprieve.

The roast was overdone.

"He's right you know," Sara said as they walked up Court Street. "If it wasn't for my work—and yours—I don't think I'd want to live here."

"Go to the country, maybe?" Madden asked. "Maybe build a solar roof and a windmill and live off the land?"

"You could do it. After all, you're supposed to be a talented engineer."

"An engineer, right. Not a farmer. A civilized man, not a rustic."

"You can be rustic enough at times," she countered. As they went down into the Boro Hall subway station, she still was laughing at him. Madden glanced at his watch. It was eleven twenty-three.

He had no premonition, nothing in the way of advance warning, no idea at all that he'd never hear Sara laugh again.

# THREE

There were four of them. They got on the subway at Fulton, directly entering the car in which Madden and Sara were the only passengers. Both of them were sampling the books she'd bought, Madden pondering over one of the great Leonardo's more complicated sketches which the editor's notes didn't do much to uncomplicate. But even as the door closed and the train again began moving northward, Madden knew something was wrong. His eyes had hardly lifted from the printed page when the hairs on the back of his neck told him something was *dangerously* wrong.

There were four of them. All black, all young, maybe an average age of eighteen. One of them wore a wild pink cap, a wide "bopper" kind of thing. That, more than anything, Madden remembered later. That and the long switchblade the kid with the cap had.

Madden both saw and heard it snap open. He put out a protective hand before Sara's chest. He heard her sharp intake of breath, then heard the book she was reading slip to the floor of the car. He didn't see her face, though. He was occupied with the faces of the four—more especially the face of the one with the knife, the one who spoke.

"No trouble now, hear? All we wants is your money, just the cash. No cards, nothing else, just—"

That was as far as he got before Madden launched himself off the seat. He was as surprised as the knifeman to feel the doubled-up fist of his right hand slam into the other's stomach. *How long had it been since he'd actually struck someone?*

But the question, although asked somewhere to the rear of his brain, couldn't be answered, not then. Madden's conscious mind was occupied with other things, frantically occupied. Not even Sara's sudden scream behind him made him take his eyes from that flashing knifeblade as he drove his left fist into the face of the one who held it. It was only as the force of the blow catapulted the knifeman from before him and sent the black youth crashing to the other side of the car that Madden turned, prepared to deal with the next of the four.

But they too were prepared, or one of them was. Something heavy and cylindrical blurred through the space above Madden's head, something wielded by the one now closest to him. Reflexively, he put his hands up to protect himself, but in doing so he left his mid-section unprotected.

He saw the heavy boot coming, but wasn't able to move, not fast enough. He felt the fire burst in his gut as the boot slammed home, then he heard Sara's hysterical shriek. Then, as he pawed the air, trying to grab something by which he could shove himself forward, toward where his wife—

Good Christ! *Sara—*

The scene was as if frozen in time. The one black who had been standing before her now stood to her left, a knife in his right hand, her purse in the other. The purse was upside down, its contents spilling out, they too seemingly frozen in midair. Sara—

Her eyes were open wide in terror, her face transfigured into a pale white bloodless color. Madden's focus shifted from her face to her chest where the material of her coat was sliced horizontally and from which already rivulets of red were forming.

*"Sara!"*

His single word had the effect of starting the flow of time again. He saw now that the position of the knife in the black's hand was preparatory for another swing. He saw that swing begin.

And then that heavy cylinder—that thick metal pipe—crashed into the side of his ear. An explosion of multicolored lights detonated behind his eyes as if the firecrackers of Chinese New Year were lighting up some darkened sky. He fell forward, knowing he had to get his hands in some kind of position to break that fall. But his hands wouldn't move, he simply couldn't control them. He felt the surface of the car floor against his face. Then he heard Sara scream again.

Her other screams had been bad enough, but this one was such a combination of horror and agony as he'd never heard before in his life, a sound which he thought was impossible for one human being to utter and impossible for another human to hear without crossing the borderline to the madness which touched the sound itself. The moaning scream remained in his ears, it was a sound which seemed as if it wasn't ever going to stop. He had to help her—*he had to help his wife*—

He somehow managed to get his hands under his shoulders, and somehow also managed to raise himself almost to his knees. His eyes at first refused to focus. And then they did.

*Good God!*

Her forehead glistened with the blood which covered it, blood which flowed into her eyes and down her cheeks, blood which flowed from under the loose horrible flap of skin which paralleled her hairline. There was a second source of blood, at least a second.

Sara's throat—

Scramblingly, Madden tried to push himself forward. Then, amidst the screaming sound, he heard someone laugh. A heavy pressure came suddenly to the base of his skull and he felt himself falling again. Falling down, down past the level of the train floor, down past the tracks, down into some bottomless pit. The sounds of agony and those of laughter were suddenly nothing more than echoes from some distant place.

And then they weren't even that, and the blackness itself enveloped him in its deathly silence.

"Sara . . . Sara . . ."

There was a voice in the blackness now, one he thought he recognized. As the blackness turned into a slightly lighter shade, his mind struggled to identify that voice, but the pain was intolerable. His head seemed blasted into a thousand fragments, but still that same voice continued to echo around inside his skull, to make the pain worse.

The voice was his own, he recognized that at the same time the gray behind his eyes lifted just enough so that he could see the dim outlines of a small face before his own.

"Sara . . ."

But it wasn't Sara. It was a woman in white. She wore an odd pointed cap. "Rest easy, Mr. Madden," she said, then she seemed to be talking to somebody else in

30

the room—the strange white room. "He's coming around . . ."

But not fully so, the voices all sounded as if from a distance. There was still a blur in front of Madden's eyes in addition to other images. One image he thought he recognized as it was shoved up close to him. A silver badge. He focused in on that and held his eyes open. The image sharpened, as did that of the face behind the hand which displayed the badge.

"Can you answer some questions, Mr. Madden?"

"Sara . . ."

"Stay lying back there, Mr. Madden. You took a nasty crack on the head."

"My wife . . ."

"Please, Mr. Madden. If you can just—"

*"My wife!"*

Hands restrained him now, more than one pair, even though he could not mentally connect arms and faces to them. He recognized now that he was in a bed or on some sort of table. It was a hospital or emergency ward, it had to be. There was a cabinet with a red cross on the glass, and there was on the wall across the room a chart with letters, the top one a large black *E.*

"Mr. Madden, you *must*—"

"My wife. Where is my wife?"

"She . . . she's across the hall . . . in the room across the hall."

Exactly who was doing the talking now, he couldn't tell. He didn't care. "I—I want to talk to—they were *cutting*—"

A pair of hands from somewhere gripped his arms tightly.

"Mr. Madden, please don't excite—"

But he stopped listening to that voice. It was the

31

other voices, those of the two or three others whose dimming-clearing outlines came to him, they were the ones he was trying to hear.

"No . . . can't tell him now. Later, when . . ."

"But he *is* the woman's husband."

". . . his condition . . ."

"If I were in this man's shoes . . ."

"You're not, Sergeant."

"If I *were,* though, I'd want—"

"I'm not all that sure that *I* would."

*"My wife!"* Madden roared. With a burst of strength he sat straight up, lurching his arms, freeing them from the hands which had held him, jumping free from the table or bed or whatever it was and slashing through the opening—and toward the door which suddenly was open. Another woman in white stood there, a young woman with long blonde hair. Madden stopped.

"S-Sara?"

And then he knew it wasn't, but it was too late. The hands from behind were on him again and something stung his left arm. He saw the glint of the needle, his eyes turning to plead with the badge, wherever it was. It no longer was in sight, but only one of the people around him was wearing something other than hospital white.

And then he stopped seeking because he couldn't remember what it was he had been looking for. Yes—yes, he did. Sara. He was looking for Sara, he was looking for looking for looking looking looking look—looking . . . for . . . Sarasarasarasara . . .

The two syllables whispered in the darkness again and again. Over and over Madden tried to make sense of them, tried to grip on just one of the syllables to stop the passage of soft sound through the corridors of his mind, but he could not do so. One of the syllables would not hold without the one which followed, and he didn't have the mental strength for two. But what could it mean, this repetitious two syllable sound?

Sa Ra.

Sa . . . ra.

Sa–ra.

Sara.

*Sara.*

*He was looking for Sara.*

He sat up, his mind still foggy, still swimming within some unseen swirls within the darkness which surrounded him. He was—

Where? A hospital. Yes, that's where he was. That's where he was now. Earlier, he had been at Sara's sister's place, and then—

Sara!

*"She's . . . across the hall."*

Somebody had said that, somebody had said that his wife was in the room across the hall. Who?

It didn't matter. What mattered was that Sara was in the room across the hall. She was there and she needed him. He couldn't fail her. He was her husband and he loved her and she—she was the most precious thing in the world.

It took a while, a struggling while, but he made it off the bed with his naked feet firmly on the floor. It took a while longer, but eventually he was at the door to the room and turning the knob.

The hall outside was lighted and it was silent. It also was completely empty. Carefully, slowly edging himself through the doorway, he slid his feet across the corridor and to the door of the room directly opposite.

That knob turned too. As he pushed the door open—

33

The bright light from within pierced his eyes with a stinging pain. Moving blindly inside, he leaned against the door with his back and heard the latch click behind him. It took his sight a few moments to accustom itself to the light, but when it did—

It was a small room, smaller than his own.

There was only one bed, except it wasn't a bed.

It was a kind of table. On that table . . .

There was someone. Someone who was completely covered with a sheet, from toe to top of head.

"No," he whispered. "No!"

*They only do that when you're dead.*

No, it couldn't be the right room. It couldn't—

*She's across the hall . . .*

Oh, God. No, please God . . .

He didn't want to move an inch, didn't want to get any nearer to that table with the body covered by the sheet. But there was nothing else he could do, nothing.

He didn't take a breath until the fingers of his right hand grasped the top end of the sheet. Even then he didn't breathe. Not until he gently lifted the end and pulled it back. He breathed then.

He screamed then.

*"My God, my God. Sara—oh my God!"*

He stood, the sheet still in his raised right hand, his eyes focused on a face he recognized but did not recognize. A mutilated face. One which had been so terribly beautiful this very morning, this very evening, but now—now a face which, because of some brightly shining knife—

*"Mr. Madden!"*

The voice came from behind him. He turned to see the white uniform and the woman's face above it. The woman looked frightened. He didn't want her to be frightened.

"Please," he said. "Please . . ."

The light of the room suddenly was fading. He didn't want that, not now. "Please," he said again. "Please don't . . . don't go away."

Was it Sara he was pleading with? Was it the nurse? Was it the light? He began to ask himself, to try to sort things out, but the light continued to fail, the whites before his eyes turning into deeper and deeper shades of gray, slipping everything—including himself—into that familiar black nowhere . . .

"You will be all right, Mr. Madden."

The doctor was a small bald-headed man in his late fifties, a complete physical opposite to the bull-shaped nurse whose face Madden had first seen upon awakening. He knew it was daylight from the sun coming through the curtains, but there had been no "good morning" from the stolid lady in white, nor was there now from the small-boned hairless man.

In that they were alike. They also shared the same look about the eyes—an empty, non-communicative look which contrasted to the fact that the doctor was speaking words intended to communicate.

"You've sustained a pretty severe concussion but X-rays show no further complications. As long as you take it easy . . ."

The words. He heard them without hearing, without their registering on his brain matter. His hands gripped the sides of the bed as the doctor talked. For how long the man went on Madden didn't know, but he knew the subject had switched to his wife. It could have been just two or three words or two or three sentences or it could have been the standard sermon endorsed by the full contingent of hospital chaplains of whatever faith. He felt the numbing take over his mind and his body, felt the complete emptying of everything of substance from within the shell which his body had become. There was nothing within that shell—nothing. Nothing at all but a terrible moaning cry:

"Sara—oh my God!"

The policeman's name was Delancy. He was fat. He wore plain clothes and probably was a sergeant. Madden still was having difficulty sorting things out. He remembered the man said he was on robbery detail—or was it homicide? In any case he used the words *robbery* and *homicide*. He mentioned a precinct number as he flashed his badge, doing both as he offered Madden a ride uptown.

Ride uptown, Madden repeated mentally. Sure ... the subway, maybe ...

But he said nothing, just nodded. Once in the unmarked car, Delancy was silent for the first two blocks. Madden got the impression that the man was mentally counting to a hundred, that maybe some sort of rule in the book, based on psychological testing or data collected from homicide division experience over the years, said that the survivor should be given a full one hundred seconds before getting down to the dull routine of questioning. Or maybe the number was a hundred and fifty or two hundred.

"You have any relatives in town, Mr. Madden?"

"My wife has a sister, in Brooklyn," *Has*. Madden closed his eyes. It was the wrong tense. He opened them and waited for Delancy to comment on his mistake, but the cop acted as if he hadn't heard it. No. he'd heard it.

He'd probably heard this kind of thing before, many times before.

"If you let me have her name and address, I'll have her contacted. That is, if you'd like me to."

"No. I'll take care of it," Madden said dully. Then: "Did you get the bastards?"

"Sir?"

"The ones responsible for—" But he couldn't complete his sentence.

"We're going to need your help for that, Mr. Madden. Tomorrow, maybe, after you've rested, there are some pictures we'd like you to have a look at."

"You haven't caught—"

"No, sir. Not yet. They left the train somewhere before Fourteenth Street. The patrolman on the train—"

"There was a patrolman *on* the train?"

Delancy nodded grimly. "He was the one who found you and—" He broke off, seeming to become suddenly occupied with the guiding of the automobile.

*And my wife,* Madden's mind completed the sentence. He now tried to recall her face, her beautiful laughing face, but he couldn't. Then he stopped trying, because he knew that if he were successful in recalling that image, he'd scream. He knew he'd get to that state, but let it come when he was better prepared for it, when his subconscious decreed that he was ready.

But for now there was something else his conscious mind was pressing upon him.

"You—*haven't* caught them?"

"No, Mr. Madden. We have too little to go on. Like I said, the train patrolman—"

"I didn't see any cop—policeman on that train at all."

Delancy shrugged. He didn't mean to, maybe, but he

37

did. He said, "I wasn't told his beat. Maybe he got on after—after it happened."

"Yeah," Madden said. "When the train was in safe territory." He no sooner said it than he realized he shouldn't have said it. "Look, I'm sorry. I didn't mean—"

"It's okay, Mr. Madden. I understand."

He understood. Maybe he did. Maybe he understood all too well, having had to hear it too many times.

"When—" Madden began, then he stopped, thinking to himself that he didn't want to hear the answer. But he went ahead anyway. "When do you think you will get them?"

"Hard to tell. Maybe I'll have a better idea after you go over the photgraphs I want you to see. Right now, we've got little to go on. That reminds me. Your wallet."

Madden reached into his breast pocket. His wallet wasn't there. Then he saw why. Delancy had reached into his coat pocket and was handing it to him.

"They left it behind—your cards and things scattered in the car. We had it all checked out for fingerprints— everything—but we don't figure on much coming from it. Oh, you'll notice they did take time to clean you out of folding money."

"It wasn't much," Madden said absently. What was he saying? Why were they talking about money? Why now, of all times—

"They took your wife's purse with them," Delancy was saying. "They always do, I guess because they figure women have little compartments where they hide bills and such. If she was carrying a checkbook, I'd no-

38

tify your bank if I were you—same thing with any charge accounts she might have—"

"Sergeant—"

Delancy nodded again. "Sorry. I shouldn't be saying all this to you now. I can understand what you're going through and—"

"No. I mean, that's all right. I appreciate—" He stopped. He didn't appreciate anything, not now, but he knew the man was trying to do his job, and he knew that he was also trying to be helpful.

"Did you talk to Sara? Did you ask her—"

"We tried, Mr. Madden. There wasn't much time and—she didn't want to talk to us."

Was that a nice way of saying that she couldn't—that she was too busy screaming with fright and horror?

"She was worried, sir," Delancy went on. "She refused to believe that you were all right."

Madden echoed the word. "Worried. About me . . . " He thought about it. Then, to change his line of thinking, he asked, "Are you married?"

"Me?" Delancy asked. And a sudden tautness came over the man. "No . . . I'm not married, Mr. Madden."

"Neither am I," Madden said. "Not anymore. They've fixed that for—"

And it was then and there, in an unmarked police car heading north on Manhattan Island, that Joe Madden broke down. The hands he held over his face weren't somehow strong enough. They couldn't suppress the sobbing sounds which were coming from his mouth. They couldn't hold back the tears which were drenching his cheeks. For they too were shaking and wouldn't stay in place.

"Sergeant . . . I'm sorry . . . "

"There's no need to be sorry, Mr. Madden."

39

"But there is. A man . . . doesn't . . . " he sobbed.

Delancy was quiet for a time. Madden's hands blocked any view of the expression on the man's face, but then the policeman broke the silence with a low rumbling tone.

"Yes, he does, Mr. Madden. A man cries. When there's reason, there's nothing else he can do."

# FOUR

Somehow, he didn't know how, he made it from the car across the sidewalk to his building. Delancy offered to come with him, but he shook his head no. "I'll be all right," he insisted, but couldn't look at the man when he said it. He *couldn't*. But Delancy didn't pull away from where he'd double-parked until the outside apartment building door had closed behind Madden.

He half fell across the terrazzo floor of the small lobby, and his thumb came in contact with the up button of the elevator on first try. *Please, God, let it be empty. No people, not now.*

But there were people. Two women and two small children in prams. He tried to avoid looking at them as they exited the car, but he couldn't help but notice them and how they exchanged glances upon seeing him. He and Sara had exchanged similar glances when coming unexpectedly upon some drunk on the streets.

Sara . . .

He clasped his right hand to his mouth and stumbled into the car. No sooner had the door closed than he felt the taste of vomit in his mouth. *God no, not here!*

He swallowed hard, his insides groaning with agony under the strain he was subjecting them to. But they withstood the pressure until the door opened at the third

41

floor and he staggered to his door and turned the knob. The door was locked—of course it was locked!—but the fact struck him as being somehow humorous, and amidst the sobs he heard coming from his throat, there came a savage laugh. Lock them out, Joe—lock them out now that it's too goddamned late!

He looked at his left hand and was surprised to see the key ring there. It was sheer conditioning. As the elevator car rose, his left hand automatically had dipped into the proper trousers pocket and clasped around the keys. And almost automatically now, the same hand was inserting the proper key into its lock.

It was in the hallway to the apartment, the door closed behind him, that he doubled over and his guts pushed out everything they could. By the time he had control over himself he was kneeling on the hardwood floor, his knees soaked in his own internal stench. *Christ—Christ!*

And his ears were ringing.

Because the telephone was ringing.

There in the living room it sat, on its stand—a refinished vaudeville trouper's trunk which had cost Sara many hours of hard labor. How she carried on the day she brought it home. "You don't see the *possibilities*," she had told Madden who, his eye jaundiced toward her big find—

Sara. *My God—Sara!*

But his hand was on the telephone now. He lifted the mouthpiece.

He recognized the voice, an urgent voice:

"Joe? Joe—are you there?" Crosby asked into the void.

"I'm ... here," he managed to say. He was on his knees, still—or again. He didn't know which, but somehow he had crossed the distance between the hallway and telephone. "I'm here, Hal."

"But why aren't you *here,* Joe? For Christ's sake, don't you know that Grossman—" And then the voice stopped. When it resumed, the tone was completely different. "Joe—is something the matter?"

"Sara," Madden said.

Crosby repeated the name, as if speculatively. As he did so, Madden realized that Hal and Sara had met only once, at the last office Christmas party. Hal lived in the suburbs. Jersey, up north, Connecticut, Long Island—somewhere out there. Who the hell knew? And who the hell knew what Crosby's wife's name was? He didn't—not now, at least. Maybe if he had time to think, maybe if his mind was receptive to recalling past conversations—

Evidently, Crosby's mind was.

"Sara—your wife? Joe, what's happened?"

"She's dead, Hal. They killed her."

He hung up.

He had managed to move no further than three feet from the phone—to the wingback chair by its side—when again he heard the thing ring.

Again he picked it up without speaking. Again it was Crosby.

"Joe . . . you . . . "

There was an uncomfortable pause. Crosby coughed. "You're not kidding, are you? I mean, what you said just now—"

"She's dead," Madden said. In saying it, he seemed to be some kind of robot. No. Two robots. One watching and storing the data that the other was delivering. "My wife is dead, Hal."

There was a silence, so much of one that Madden began to think the line had malfunctioned. Then:

"Joe . . . what can I . . ."

"Nothing, Hal. Nobody can do nothing."

"Joe—where are you? No, that's stupid. I *know* where you are. Can I come up? I mean, do you want somebody—" And suddenly Hal Crosby was talking like an electric typewriter gone amok. "Joe, listen. I'll tell the old man, and then I'll grab a cab and—look, stay where you are and—"

"I'm not going anywhere, Hal." He felt as if he were a corpse, saying those words. Not going anywhere. It struck him—stupidly so, maybe—that the phrase also might be indicative of his professional progress. Don't we talk about a man "moving" in his career? We do. "Going places" has to do as much with advancement on the job or at one's profession as it does with geographical movement. Job. What the hell *was* his job? Who the hell was this voice on the other end of the telephone?

"No," he said sullenly. "Don't come up, Hal. I don't want—"

"But what happened? An accident? Joe—"

"Don't, Hal. Don't say anything. Anything."

"Look, Joe. I'll—"

"Don't."

He hung up. Then he sat staring at the phone, waiting for it to ring again. He could picture Hal frantically dialing his number a third time. But the ring didn't come. No, probably Hal had rushed into the old man's office. After a couple of minutes, then the phone would ring and it would be Chilton himself. Chilton, wondering what he could do . . .

He could continue to wonder, Madden decided. He took the receiver off the hook. As he did so, he saw the dried vomit on his hand. The smell of his insides seemed to bombard his nostrils, and his head reeled. He needed a drink, needed one real bad.

He had the Johnnie Walker in the water tumbler and all he needed now was the ice.

It was on the refrigerator door, the note among four others, all fastened to the door by small unpainted magnets. He felt his heart stop beating as he saw Sara's handwriting on the small pieces of paper—felt-tip pen, green, on torn notepad sections:

*Carrots,* said one. The others:

*Candles.* She was a candle nut, loved them brilliantly blazing around the table at mealtime.

*KT's birthday.* KT? He didn't know any KT who was having a birthday. Probably somebody at her office.

And then the topmost note:

*Jean's Mon. nite.*

Madden closed his eyes. He should have had that cop call Jean. But he hadn't, so now it was up to him. He turned from the refrigerator without opening the door, his quest for ice having been forgotten. Back in the living room, he looked at the telephone, then sat down into the chair next to it. He took half the glass of Scotch in his first swallow. It burned his raw throat on the way down, bringing tears to his eyes. Sure, it was the Scotch that did it, nothing else . . .

He picked up the receiver and pushed down the button. His right index finger was poised above the dial when he recognized he had no idea of his sister-in-law's number. Besides, she wouldn't be at home now, she'd be at work. And he didn't know where she worked, he didn't even know what kind of job she had. Secretarial, he thought, but he was never interested enough to find out, and besides she never did much talking. It was always Dan doing the talking.

Then he remembered the book Sara kept.

He knew where it was. In their bedroom, in the low Danish modern chest of drawers. Right hand side, top drawer—Sara's "important paper file." Among the important papers, a white tattered little book with addresses and phone numbers. It was there, all right, it had to be. Except he didn't want to get it. He didn't want to see their bedroom now, not now.

He drained the rest of the glass, then walked to the kitchen where he'd left the Scotch bottle and refilled the tumbler, this time all the way to the top. He took a healthy mouthful, noticing that as it gravitated down through his system it didn't burn quite as much any more. He steeled himself and walked down the narrow hallway to the bedroom.

He swallowed hard at the sight of the unmade bed where just last night—no, it had been the night before . . .

Blocking out the rest of the room mentally, he opened the top right drawer. The book was in plain sight. Thank God it was. If he had been forced to move any of her other things . . .

Back out in the living room now, back in the chair next to the telephone, he thumbed through the pages of the book. The print seemed to blur out the names of friends they knew but he now couldn't place. Then he found it. Jean's home number and work number. And Dan's work number.

Dan. Yes, he should call Dan, not Jean. Let her husband break the news that her sister was—

Let him break the goddamned news.

The woman who answered seemed irked that he'd called. "Just a minute, I'll see if he's accepting calls."

A hell of a way to run a sales-oriented business, Madden thought to himself. "Tell him—tell him it's his brother-in-law."

"I'll tell him."

There was a pause worth three swallows of Johnnie Walker then:

"Joe? Is that you, Joe?"

"Yeah, Dan. It's Joe, I—"

The laugh from the other end sounded like an avalanche. "Jesus! What's the occasion? I mean, let's face it—this is the first time you ever bothered to call me at work. The first time you ever called me at all, if I remember right, and I do. What's the big deal?"

"There's something . . . something urgent . . ."

"Urgent? You don't sound so urgent, Joe. Matter of fact, you sound a little smashed. Okay, what's up?"

"Sara—"

Later, he couldn't recall the words he used to get the message across. But he did get it across that he knew, because he remembered Dan's hushed question:

"Jesus! What in hell am I going to tell Jean?"

"Tell her," Madden said heavily, "tell her she's lucky."

"Lucky?"

"Lucky," he repeated. "Jean's still alive."

He no sooner had hung up the phone when it rang. It was Chilton's secretary, an ancient creature whose name was Blanche and who asked him with a nervous voice to please hold on. "Mr. Chilton's been trying to reach you!" she said, almost hysterically.

And then Chilton himself:

"Joe—what's happened? Hal said—"

Madden cut him off. It was easy, going through the

general points again. He'd just done it, after all, and this time he seemed to recall with the kind of memory which was his stock and trade the exact words he had used with Dan. When he was finished, he saw that there was no more Scotch in his glass.

Chilton did not say anything right away. For a few seconds, Madden wondered whether the old man was still on the line. But he was:

"Joe, this is horrible."

"Yeah, horrible," Madden repeated.

"Look, Joe. I know there's not much I or anybody else here can do at a time like this, but I also want you to know something else. I value you as an employee—a damned good one—and as, I hope, a friend."

"Thanks. I guess I need a friend right now."

"But not a friend butting in—correct?"

"Correct."

"Joe, you've got enough to think about right now, enough to worry about. Don't think or worry about your work. Take as much time as you need. When you decide to come back—"

"That's generous of you—"

"Not as generous as you think. You'll be back faster than you think right now, Joe. And I'm telling you that the faster it happens the better it will be. What's done is done and there's nothing you can do about it. I hope that, since I'm an old man, you'll listen to me and maybe even believe that I know what I'm talking about. I lost my wife some time ago. Not under anything like the circumstances which you—" He stopped, then went on: "But ... I know the feeling of loss. And I know that it wasn't long before I had to get back to work. To restore some kind of balance as it were. Joe, are you listening to me?"

48

"Listening."

"Then have another drink. I don't think you've had enough yet."

When the old man's voice was gone, Madden thought about what he'd said, the last thing he'd said. Chilton was right—and Chilton had the reputation of hating booze. The man didn't drink at all.

*Now* he didn't drink, but then? When he felt the same kind of loss that Madden—

No. It wasn't the same. By Chilton's own admission, it wasn't the goddamned same!

But the advice was good regardless.

His watch said it was four thirty-five when he staggered to the door to answer the bell. Their faces refused to come into clear focus, but he let them in anyway. Jean and Dan.

Jean: "Good lord, Joe, Dan said—"

Dan: "I told her the whole thing. I thought it best."

Jean: "Where *is* she, Joe? I mean, where is she now?"

Dan: "Jean's concerned about the funeral arrangements. I tried to tell her it was none of her business, but—"

"Joe—what about the arrangements?"

"Have a drink," Madden said.

"A *drink?*" Jean's little dried up face—dried up, yes. He'd never thought about her that way exactly, but that was what she was. Not only her face, but her insides as well. Dried-up. A goddamned prune at thirty-one or two or three or whatever the hell age she was.

"A drink?" she repeated. "At a time like this—"

Madden's voice was hard. "I lost my wife today, baby."

"Your wife? You've known Sara for how long? How

49

long, I ask you?" Her face now was alternating between blood red and bone white. "She's been my sister for a lot longer, Joe. You've got to admit that, you've got to recognize that."

Madden didn't comment. He could think of no comment. There was therefore no way of stopping the continual outpouring as the presence of Jean and Dan pushed him back into his living room.

"Now, as to the funeral arrangements, I will—"

"There will be no funeral," Madden said.

"No—"

"None. Sara and I both . . ."

His voice trailed off. He remembered that day in Central Park when they made the decision. It was an easy decision then, both of them on that warm September day, looking across the lake at the weather forecast castle, whatever its name was. They had seen, minutes before, a little child who might have been crippled from polio or some birth defect, and Sara, the fading rays of the sun shining through her golden hair, her lovely soft golden hair, had said it. "When I die, Joe—"

"Die?" he had asked. "That's a long time coming."

"When I die," she'd repeated, "I don't want any fancy burial. I want to leave my body to medical science. I really do. Would you mind that?"

He had laughed. "Mind? Do you think I want you buried in some plot that I had to put flowers on every anniversary of our wedding—or on your birthday? Hell, yes. A great idea!"

But she had been serious, very serious. She'd located the proper agencies and signed whatever papers were necessary. He'd even put his own signature to identical papers. "Hell," he said, "I'll be long dead before you— dead and buried."

"That's the whole point, Joe. Dead, yes, but not buried. Even after death, part of us will be able to help people. I want that for us, both of us. Besides—I don't want to have to screw up my afternoons by having to remember to put flowers on your grave, either."

They had laughed about it then. And why not? *Then* they had decades ahead of them. Now . . .

"No burial?" Jean said. "It's sacrilegious!"

He looked at her, trying to comprehend what she was saying. She did her best to make sure he did:

"There has to be a burial—and a proper funeral, too! Sara had a proper religious upbringing, no matter what kind of atheistic things you taught her, Joe Madden! I insist—"

"She wanted it this way, Jean," he said. "It was her decision, and I'll abide by it. She wanted it—"

*"Wanted?"*

It wasn't Jean who repeated the word, but a male voice. Madden remembered there was somebody else in his apartment. He turned to face Dan.

"Wanted?" Dan said again. The look on his face was strange—unpleasant. "What the hell do you know what she wanted? I suppose you're going to tell me that she *wanted* to die, that she *wanted* to get sliced up by that bastard's knife!"

Madden's head felt suddenly as if it was going to crack wide open. "Dan, what the hell are you saying—"

"I'm saying that you're one hell of a somebody to be standing here saying what Sara would have liked or what she wanted. You—"

Jean said from behind Madden: "Dan—"

He waved her to silence. "No, damn it, I'm going to say what I'm going to say. You, Joe—what goddamned right do you have saying anything about what Sara

51

wanted? She didn't want to die, you know that and so do I. If I was there, it wouldn't have happened, I'll say that—but you! What the hell were you doing while they were killing Sara? Where were you when—"

As Madden lunged, there was little logic or rationality to his move. All he knew was that he had to shut up that ugly face before him. He heard the scream of the woman behind him, but it didn't matter. All that mattered was stopping those goddamned words, those goddamned accusing words—

He felt his right fish smash into face, he felt the left fist crack into the other side of Dan's head. He saw astonishment and he saw blood and then he saw the bigger man go down. He heard the woman scream his name once, twice. Then he felt her frail hands trying to grasp his arms—

"Please, Joe! Don't hit him again! He didn't mean—"

She stopped when he turned around.

"He didn't mean," Madden said dully. "Then he shouldn't have said."

"He—"

But Madden's eyes were now on the other man again, watching like the eyes of some starved hawk for Dan to make a sudden aggressive move. Dan moved, but it was a movement which looked as if he were shrinking. Actually he was sliding backward away from Madden, so that he was sure to be out of fist range when he rose.

When he did rise, his face wore a stupid grin.

"Hey, Joe—what the hell? Why should we fight? I ain't done nothing to you. I can understand how maybe—"

"Shut up, Dan."

To Madden's surprise it wasn't his voice which issued the command. Dan also was surprised.

"Jean—"

"Please. Shut your mouth. Can't you see what Joe is going through?"

She didn't wait for an answer, but instead grasped Madden's right hand. It still was curled into a tight fist. The recognition of that made him relax. *Christ! I am not a violent man, I've never—*

"Joe. I'll call you tomorrow morning all right?"

"Jean—"

"I know, Joe. I'm sorry for—all this, all of what happened. Can I call you in the morning?"

Morning. Yes, there would be a morning. There would be a tomorrow when he would wake up from a night's sleep and he would look for—

But she wouldn't be there.

"Jean." Just the name, that's all he could say. But somehow the little face which he always had considered to be dried-up seemed to understand.

"Tomorrow, Joe. I'm . . . I'm sorry."

And then she seemed to pick up her husband as if he'd weighed nothing, shushing his mouth which wanted to say something to silence, and leading the big man to the apartment door.

"Joe?" she said.

"Yeah, tomorrow."

"I'll call about ten. Be sure to lock the door after we leave?"

He looked at her uncomprehendingly. Then Dan, his hand to his jaw, spoke.

"You better do like she says. Lock it tight. Tight as hell."

53

# FIVE

There was a ringing in his ears ... bells ringing ... Church bells, maybe, like for a wedding. Sara and he hadn't had a church wedding, but now they were ringing the bells ...

He turned to his right in the bed. "Sara, baby, listen to the—"

But she wasn't there. Naturally.

He looked to the clock at his left. Nine forty. Hell! He'd forgotten to set the alarm again and—"

The damned telephone.

He called out to Sara, loud enough to make sure she could hear him from the kitchen. "Hey, baby—answer it out there and tell them—"

He was sitting up in the bed, his head swimming from Scotch hangover, but not swimming so badly that he couldn't remember.

Sara was not in the kitchen.

Sara was in some slab at some morgue—or by now at some medical research facility.

He was alone.

And the telephone was ringing.

He picked it up. "Hello."

"Joe?" A female voice. Jean's. "I promised I'd call. If it's too early—"

54

"It's early," he said. Then he hung up the phone. Early, hell! Why couldn't they let him sleep?

They?

Right, they! All of them. All of them out there who— Unfair. Joe. Unfair as hell. Sleep on it.

He did.

The bedside clock said the time was two or three minutes after eleven when he awoke. It was again the ringing of the telephone which woke him. And again, as if in some trance, he spoke into the detached mouthpiece.

"Hello."

"Mr. Madden. This is Leo Delancy. Sergeant Leo Delancy. You remember me from yesterday?"

"I remember," Madden said. His swimming mind told him that he probably did.

"Good. I told you that I wanted to talk to you today. Show you some pictures. How do you feel?"

"Lousy."

"Me too. Suppose I grab some coffee and stop for some hamburgers. Would you feel like company—with coffee and hamburgers?"

Madden suddenly realized he was hungry, savagely so. But—

"I don't feel so good," he said.

"Me neither. Let's the two of us talk about it. You like onions and relish?"

"How's that?"

"On your hamburgers. And how many you want? But before you answer that, remember that it's taxpayers' dough you're spending."

"Three. Three big ones. Onions, pickles, everything—and screw the taxpayers."

"Not all of them, Mr. Madden. After all, you're a taxpayer. See you in a half hour."

"Wait a second," Madden said. "Delancy—you pay taxes too, right?"

"Afraid so."

Madden laughed. "Then get two orders of french fries to go with those burgers. Unless you want some, in which case you'd better get three."

A half hour. Madden got up and headed toward the bathroom. It was then he noticed that he still wore the clothes he had worn yesterday—in fact the clothes he had put on the day before yesterday. Noting that, he didn't want to go into the bathroom at all. Because the whole thing hit him again. Two days ago, they had been in such a hurry to get out of here . . .

Her bathrobe was in the middle of the floor. Her bath towel was next to it . . .

Sara. You're dead, Sara. I tried to help, baby, honest I did, but . . .

No. If he followed that line of thought he'd be a basket case. No. Delancy was going to be here in a half hour, and he had to get ready. At the very least he had to brush his teeth . . .

Somehow he managed that chore. But that was all he could manage. Once in the bathroom he had a chance to assess himself. The mirror over the double sinks said part of it. He looked like hell. He needed a shave badly. His clothes were rumpled so much that he looked like some Bowery bum, if the Bowery was the main place for bums these days. What did somebody like Joe Madden, respectfully employed consulting engineer, know about things like that?

Screw it.

Screw the fact that he smelled, too. Because he did smell—he smelled like blood and puke and worse. But what difference did it make? He was after all in his own goddamned apartment. *His* apartment! And if Sergeant Delancy didn't like the way he smelled or looked, then it was tough crap . . .

But Madden himself didn't like the way he smelled or looked. Nor did he like the way his mouth tasted, even after he'd tried to scour it to some kind of neutrality with a toothbrush he'd wielded with a self-destructive vengeance.

Coffee. That was what he needed. It was morning, after all, and what else was morning if not a time for—

He turned around toward the bathroom door, half expecting a lovely nude girl to be standing there with his steaming cup. He closed his eyes. No, she'd never be there again— *never again.*

All right. One part of his mind started trying to talk sense to another part. You're not a damned child. You can make your own coffee. You did make your own, those years between Helen and . . .

He left the bathroom and went into the kitchen. He had the water in the percolator and was looking for the coffee can in the cupboard when the phone rang. He picked up the living room extension.

It was Jean again.

"Don't hang up on me, Joe, please don't. Dan and I want to apologize for—for yesterday. Please, Joe. At a time like this there's no sense of us acting crazy, right?"

"I guess so—right."

"I called Mom and Dad last night, Joe. It killed me to have to tell them, but I thought I'd better. You really weren't in any shape to—"

"You did the right thing, Jean."

"I hope so, only—well, they're very upset."

"I understand," he said dully. *They* were upset? No, it was selfish of him to think that way. They were Sara's parents and had known her and loved her for a much longer time than he had. "I can imagine just how upset they were," he added.

"Sara's death . . . "

"I said I understood, Jean."

She paused. "And . . . and the funeral arrangements. I mean, the arrangements for *no* funeral. That had them upset too, Joe."

"I'm sorry about that," he said. He wasn't, but he said he was anyway. "Look. This is the way Sara *wanted* it. I mean—when she died . . . "

"But she never expected to die, did she, Joe? Face it, people like Sara and you—you never expect that one day—"

"That was what she wanted. She even signed a paper saying so and—"

He stopped. Christ, he'd have to try and find that piece of paper. Probably it was in the important-paper drawer somewhere. He didn't want to root through there again, but he knew he'd have to. There were other important papers in there. Insurance policies, bank books, checking account statements. He might have been the family engineer—the numbers man—but Sara had been the family bookkeeper.

"What?" he asked into the phone. Jean had been talking while he had been thinking of papers.

"I said, Joe, that Sara probably didn't even give the matter *real* thought. She never discussed the matter with me, and we were very close—"

"She gave it quite a bit of thought, Jean. She did discuss the thing with me. And we too were very close."

"Joe—I didn't mean ... What I mean is, I mean it's—after all, I don't like talking to you like this. I don't like talking to anybody like this. You're acting as if it's *my* fault that—"

And there was a silence. Madden's body was as if frozen.

Jean tried to recover. "Joe, look, I didn't mean—what I just said now, I didn't mean—"

"That it's my fault?" he asked in a tight-jawed whisper. "But it is, Jean. It's all my fault. My wife was attacked and I couldn't protect her. That's what you're thinking, isn't it? I know that's what Dan thinks."

"Joe—"

"But let me tell you what *I* think," he broke in, his voice stronger now. "You may be right in how you view me and what I did or didn't do. You may be dead right. But I don't give a good goddamn about what you think, about what Dan thinks, about what anybody thinks. Goodbye, Jean."

"Joe—"

"Jean, I don't want to be cruel to Sara's sister, not now—and not before, either. Hang up the phone or I'll have to be."

"Please, Joe—"

"All right. Baby, you're a washed-up, dried-out hag at age thirty or whatever it is you are. When you followed in your sister's footsteps and came East to the big city, you thought you'd make out just like she did. But you didn't, because you don't have one-tenth of the—"

"*Joe!*"

"Still listening? Okay. You didn't make it, so you settled on security, which in this town means marriage. How you seduced Dan into marrying you doesn't matter, because he doesn't matter very much—to me or to anybody else. So live with it, broad. Live with your own hell, but do it quietly—you caused your sister enough grief with your oh-so-sorry act. Now that she's not around to cry to, don't screw around with her arrangements for herself. Do you understand me, Jean?"

But there was no answer. She hadn't clicked off, he still could hear her breathing heavily on the other end of the line. But the conversation was over, at least it was for Madden.

"Goodbye, Jean," he said. Then he hung up.

He was in the shower when the buzzer rang. Dripping wet he traipsed through the full length of the apartment to the front door and the speaker. He pushed the button and asked who was there. Nothing answered. Whoever had rung his bell from downstairs was no longer at the call box. Unless—

Then he recognized the fact that the buzzer sound had not been that of the downstairs call box, but rather of his own door.

He opened it on the chain.

Delancy frowned at his nudity through the vertical crack. He was loaded down with brown paper bags and a thick ledger-type book. "Open it," he said. "I give you my word of honor, I won't rape you."

Madden slipped the chain and opened the door wide. "I feel kind of stupid."

"Frankly, Joe, you look kind of stupid. But, like I say, you're safe. I never screw around with naked men who haven't had their morning shave. You had your morning coffee?"

"No—but for Christ's sake, close the goddamned door!"

Delancy nodded. "Good idea. Might be some old

60

lady out there creeping around in tennis shoes, just looking for some naked, unshaved guy to sandbag. Good thinking."

He closed the door. "The food's hot and so's the coffee. Figured you wouldn't get around to brewing any."

Madden made a grab for the bag, but Delancy shifted it.

"Un-uh. Get some kind of robe or something on. This is my breakfast too, and the way you look now would turn my stomach."

Madden laughed—a real laugh. For the first time since—

As he padded back toward the bedroom, he had to admit that Sergeant Leo Delancy, fat and round and sparseheaded as he was, knew what he was doing.

But why was he doing it?

Screw it. It worked. He'd made Joe Madden laugh and had him chuckling even as he came back into the living room where the policeman had spread his breakfast treat out on the coffee table.

As Madden swallowed the first mouthful of hot coffee, he noticed that Delancy was only sipping at his own.

"Joe, there's a couple of things."

Madden halted his drinking for a couple of seconds. "More than just a couple, I hope."

"But first things first. There's the matter of the body. The hospital wants to know—"

Madden put the cup down and with two hands gripped the double burger. It didn't have the full amount of ketchup he liked to douse this sort of thing in, but he was in no mood to get up and go to the refrigerator. Let's try it the naked way this time . . .

He had it up to his mouth when he realized that Delancy had stopped abruptly in mid-sentence. Delancy, who had not yet opened his hamburger wrapping. Delancy, who was looking at him with piercing eyes.

Madden didn't take the huge bite he had planned. "Okay. What does the hospital want to know about the body?"

"Disposition," the policeman said. "If that's too technical for you, it means—"

"I know what it means, Sergeant." He took a savage bite into the double-burger, then between chews he explained how his wife's body was to be disposed of.

"I'll need the paper," Delancy said.

"I'll find it."

"More coffee?" The cop passed his unopened cup to Madden.

"Sergeant, can I ask you a personal question?"

"No."

"No?"

"No. You're a perceptive man, Joe Madden. But the question you want to ask will have to wait."

"You . . . you know what that question is?"

"I too am a perceptive man, Joe."

When the meal was finished—the policeman had eaten zero, Madden having wolfed down all of the viands the taxpayers had provided—the business began.

The book.

Picture after picture on page after page. And underneath each picture some data about crimes committed.

It took the best part of two hours, the flipping of those pages, but when the book was closed, no one individual had been identified by the only eyewitness to Joe Madden's wife's murder.

"I didn't think you'd identify them Joe," Delancy said. "Whites can identify individual blacks only rarely. A member of any race has trouble identifying a member of another. They all look the same. I know you've heard that before, and probably you've thought it something of a cliché, but it's true."

"I'd recognize one of them," Madden said. "He was the only one I saw real good, but if I ever saw him again—"

He stopped, then fingered the book.

"He wasn't there."

Delancy nodded. "Didn't expect him to be. But why is it you're so sure you could have identified—"

"Because he killed—" No, he didn't know that for sure. It could have been one of the others. They all, all four, could have been carrying knives for all he knew. But that one, he got a very good look at him. "I saw him, Sergeant. I *saw* him—and I never forget what I see."

"How do you mean, Joe?"

"Just like I said. Some people call it a photographic memory, but whatever it is, I've got it."

"The other three then—you could identify—"

"I don't know. I never really got a good look at them. I have to study a thing, a face—"

"Like you studied the faces in this book."

Madden nodded. "Like that, yes. Which—"

"Which brings you to a question you have for me."

"Right."

"I'll tell you what the question is, okay? To save time. Why, you want to know, are all those people in that book? To be in that book means that they're walking the streets. Yet the words under the pictures say they've committed crimes which should have put them away for a long, long time. Yet they're all current photos, and all the photos show them to be young. Is that your question?"

"It'll do for a start."

Delancy sighed. "I'll tell you true, Joe. The facts are—"

"Hold it. You've been calling me *Joe*. Does that mean I call you—er, whatever your first name is?"

"It's Leo. And the answer is no. Not yet. I'll tell you when, Joe."

Somehow that explanation was perfectly satsifactory to Madden—why, he couldn't have said. Even before he had the chance to think about it much, Delancy had launched into another explanation, that of the full book of faces out on the street. He began with the sheer numbers of the criminal types, numbers which far outnumbered the law enforcers. Then he moved to the trial process, which, long and arduous for the complaining party and the prosecutor, rarely ended in a stiff sentence for the accused. The courts were jammed, the prosecutors overworked, and the defending lawyers were often either the shyster type or the bleeding heart do-gooder who saw his mission to protect the rights of the bastards without giving any thought at all to the rights of the innocents who'd been mugged or raped or killed.

Madden listened until what he was listening to made him unable to finish the last bag of french fries.

"That's wrong," he said. "Wrong as hell."

"I agree," Delancy said.

"Then what are you doing about it?"

"The same thing that every honest cop is doing about it. Trying like hell to walk the tightrope that'll put those who deserve it in jail. Making sure that all the accused's rights are read to him, that it can't be said later that a confession is no good because of some technicality. You'd be surprised how many cases get thrown out just because—"

"No, I wouldn't be surprised," Madden said. "Not after seeing that book."

"And that's only one of several books, Joe. We've got other classifications, each with its own book, and other precincts have different faces—"

"And the one with the knife, the one who slashed up Sara—"

"Probably isn't in any of them. One day he probably will be, when he gets caught at something."

Delancy stood up. So did Madden.

"There's nothing more you can do, then," he said.

"Unofficially, that's the message. Officially, I'm supposed to say that we'll continue investigating, but you're smart enough to know that we've got nothing to investigate." He turned toward the door. "By the way—on my way out I'll have a word with your building superintendent. Your front doorjamb sticks so that the lock doesn't close. That's how I made it up to your front door without having to ring you from downstairs."

"I've noticed that myself."

"You're lucky. So are the other people who live in the building. Somebody with other intentions might also have noticed it, and the results—"

"Sergeant—"

"Right." Delancy turned back toward Madden. "You did have another thing you wanted to ask. That personal question."

"Maybe I shouldn't—"

"It's all right, Joe. I think maybe you've got the right to ask."

Madden thought about it. "It's just that the way you—well, the way you've acted, yesterday and today, sort of like you . . . I mean, I figure that as a cop you've run into this sort of thing a lot, but you're not as hardened about it, not really, as I thought you might—"

Delancy stopped him. His voice came as if from far away. "Her name was Margaret. She was twenty-two and we were engaged to be married. She was raped and brutally slashed. She died on the operating table."

"Sergeant, I'm sorry that I—"

"Call me Leo," the big cop said.

# SIX

It was eleven thirty or a little after when Delancy left. It hadn't taken Madden long to find the notarized paper Sara had signed donating her body to medical research, probably because the cop was with him in the bedroom while he hunted. If he had not been there, Madden probably would have lingered over items in that drawer which were of no relevance—of no relevance to anything any more . . .

Before he left, Delancy performed one more service. He found the coffee can, filled the coffeemaker, and plugged in the electric cord. As Madden stood now in the bathroom, he could hear the pop-pop-pop of the percolator as it echoed off the hallway walls. The sound somehow seemed obscene this morning, a sound which should not be allowed to continue. He was about to go out to the kitchen and unplug the thing when his eyes caught his reflection in the mirror.

Christ, he looked a mess. Hair matted, eyes almost blood-red, and a two-day-old beard that made him look like a candidate for skid row. Maybe a shave would help—

Cheer him up. That was what he was about to think, but what possibly could cheer him up now? He didn't even have the right to be cheered up. He'd been right there—right there when it had happened and he . . .

He ran the water until it got almost scalding hot, then lathered his face. He felt totally filthy, felt like showering again. He might as well. What the hell else did he have to do with his time? But first, a shave. The one act of luxury which felt so damned good every morning. A luxury, yes. That was the way he had thought about the simple act of shaving ever since that day back in May of 1951, that morning in Korea when they didn't have the opportunity to shave—and many of them never again had the chance.

It was known as Hill 800, and it was supposed to be held. But that day in May the hill was overrun by the North Koreans and their Chinese helpers. Through the day and almost all of the night, the air was so thick with lead that it was as if they were in the middle of a horizontal, metallic hailstorm. When it was over, the hill had been held, but the dead on both sides was enough to make anyone sick. The battle hardened Corporal Joseph S. Madden did not get sick. All he wanted was a shave.

There was a cleansing feeling to shaving that went far beyond what the razor did to his beard. It was as if he were somehow airing out his inner soul. For Corporal Joseph Madden had done his share of killing—before Hill 800 and afterward—but the killing always had bothered him, deep down, until that day and night had passed.

It was a goddamned war. He didn't ask to be part of it, but he was, and as long as he was he would do what he had to—and be good at it, because if he wasn't good at it, he wouldn't *be* at all . . .

And now, with half of his face shaved, Madden's

eyes were disgusted with the image of his own face. Now, more than twenty—almost twenty-five—years later maybe he didn't *deserve* to be. They—the enemy—had attacked again and he . . .

He remembered the surprise within him when he struck out, remembered how strange it felt actually to *strike* another person . . .

And that's where he had made his mistake.

They weren't persons. No, you had to think about them just as you thought about the yellow enemy in those goddamned Korean hills. They were animals, dangerous and deadly killer animals, who were to be destroyed on sight. And he, Madden, had thought of that scum with the knife as a person. A fatal mistake.

Fatal not for him, but for the woman he loved.

He looked down at the double-edged safety razor which was under the running hot water, and his fingers released it to drop to the bottom of the sink. He turned the water off and rubbed his half-shaved face free of shaving cream with the bath towel. He rubbed it hard, maybe too hard because his face hurt afterward, but that too was somehow all right. But the shave, although incomplete, was over.

Out in the kitchen now, he considered the silent coffee pot. But he couldn't touch it, his fingers somehow couldn't perform the task that had never been his, not since his marriage to Sara. He pulled the plug. In any case, he didn't feel much like coffee. His insides were churning already, and he needed no caffeine to stir up things even more.

Besides, he felt like something stronger to drink.

It was dark when he awoke. He looked at his wrist for the time, but he was wearing no watch. He was still in his bathrobe. His mouth tasted foul, his head throbbed. He was in the living room, half on and half off the couch. As he shifted himself to reach the lamp on the end table, his arm came into contact with something. Something which fell to the floor with a shattering sound.

When the light was on, he saw that it was one of Sara's fine crystal goblets, its delicate lines forever irreparable, lying there where it had struck the bottle of Johnnie Walker—

The empty bottle of Johnnie Walker which sometime during the day had overturned and spilled what had been left within it onto the living room carpet.

His bare feet avoiding the glass, he pulled himself off the couch and went toward the bedroom, flicking on lights as he did so.

The clock by the bed said it was ten thirty. Why was he so damned interested in what time it was? He had no place to go, nothing to do . . .

And the empty feeling hit him, draining him of almost the strength needed to stand. Nothing . . .

He felt it building up within him again, the uncontrollable urge to scream out at the unmade bed, the lonely apartment with its silent walls . . .

No, not absolutely silent. He could hear the city sounds from outside, those street noises of cars mostly, their engines gunning as they roared west on Seventy-seventh, their tires squealing as they reached the corner of Second Avenue, their horns blasting as other cars and pedestrians attempted to exercise their own rights upon the city streets . . .

Sounds that you forgot about, or didn't really hear, or at least sounds that your mind had long since gotten so used to that they were no more than background . . .

You forgot that there were people out there, millions of them. You forgot, because in the world's biggest city, nobody mattered. Especially when you yourself were alone . . .

Alone. He couldn't take being alone, not now. He had to get the hell out of this place. The thought of falling into that bed—the bed which had been his and Sara's—filled him with nausea which caused his head to reel. It was the booze, too, that was a part of it, but now the walls seemed actually to be shrinking, closing in on him. He had to get out!

He dressed hurriedly, not caring how he looked, wanted the cold air of the night so bad that he could taste it. Trousers on, the hell with the shorts—and a sports shirt and a jacket and then the topcoat. And then socks which might or might not have matched, and finally shoes. How long the act of dressing himself took, he couldn't say, but doing something at least did him some good. He paused only twice in his dressing, once to wash out his fuzzy tasting mouth, the second time to crack open a new bottle of liquor. They—no, *he;* it always would be just he, now—he was out of Scotch, but the bourbon he opened seemed tasteless anyway. It felt just as good going down in any case.

The night air was chilling, He shivered as it seemed to go completely through his system. He walked east, trying to walk swiftly but not completely able to do so. His head began pounding in earnest now, and his body wouldn't respond the way it wanted to. He was in bad shape, he knew that. He knew also that the best place for him at the moment was in bed, but he couldn't bring himself to go back there, not yet. Later, he'd have to, yes, but not until he'd done his best to tire out his mind and body completely. When he did have to go back, he wanted to be physically and mentally exhausted. Maybe then he would want to sleep, maybe then that bed might even look good to his depleted soul.

He walked the best he could, knowing with one part of his mind that he was staggering, knowing that when he hit the lights of First Avenue that he looked like a drunk. Hell, he was drunk, wasn't he? Didn't he in fact still have that bottle of bourbon clutched in his left hand?

He did, and he paused to drink from it. It was warmth against the cold, the only kind of warmth he wanted right now. First Avenue was all wrong for him, he saw then. There were too many lights, too many people, too much noise. He didn't want the lights which had begun to sting his eyes. Those bars and the people inside, they were having a good time or at least they thought they were having a good time. He and Sara hadn't been inside more than a couple of times, just to see . . .

Christ!

He stumbled across First, a taxi's horn blasting him for neglecting the traffic light, if in fact there was a traffic light. He thought there was, but couldn't remember now, and now that he had reached the safety of the other side, his one wish was to scurry as fast as he could into the relative darkness ahead, not to bother turning to determine whether or not there was something as meaningless as a traffic light somewhere behind. On his way back, maybe then he'd look for it. If he remembered to look for it. He hoped he wouldn't be able to remember.

"Screw traffic lights!" he said out loud, and the thickness and slowness of his own voice at first stunned him, then it pleased him. It was good. He was getting closer to the oblivion he sought.

It occurred to him that he wanted to be by the water, that maybe the sound of lapping water would do something to soothe his eyes. He had the sudden urge to know what time it was and knew that he had remembered to snap on his wristwatch, but the golden Omega did not have a luminous dial and it was too dark to make out the hands. Yet, knowing the time really wasn't of all that value, not to him, not now. It was direction that was important.

He thought he remembered turning a corner somewhere, but he wasn't sure. He shouldn't have turned a corner, not if he wanted to be by the water, but maybe he did. Maybe that was why he hadn't reached the water yet, maybe he was walking parallel to it. He was so goddamned tired, though. If he didn't reach it soon, maybe he'd better start back.

He stopped to take another swig of the bourbon and then looked around him. He was surrounded by almost total darkness, except for the lights at the ends of the long block. He didn't recognize where he was, but even if he had turned a corner—and now he thought that he had—he'd turned a second corner as well. The length of the block he was on told him that; even his fuzzy mind remembered that all blocks running east to west were twice or more as long as those going north-south. Having this one point of orientation, then, he took another drink from his bottle. He was trying to decide if it now was time to go back.

The decision was not to be his to make.

There was a voice from the darkness, one which Madden couldn't make out all that well, but one which he knew wasn't his own. At first he couldn't see the

73

speaker, then he saw the shadowy movement detach itself from an even darker space between two buildings.

The shadow moved slowly toward Madden. Madden tried to concentrate on the words being said, because he was certain now that they were intended for him. But he couldn't focus on them, nor on the face of the man who stopped before him.

All he could focus on was the knife.

They were after him again! But this time he'd show the sons of bitches!

With what Madden though was a chilling battle cry, he swung the bourbon bottle around by the neck, the horizontal arc of which was intended to end directly to the side of the knifeman's head. But the physical effort did not follow Madden's will, and he felt himself stumbling forward. He heard the other man cry out with surprise, but there was no pain in the cry. He saw for a moment a flash of light from the knifeblade, then he felt a hot burning sensation on the left side of his face. Then he felt himself falling face first to the hard pavement.

He was not conscious when the impact hit.

It was after two in the morning when they brought Delancy into the emergency room. Madden heard some of what the uniformed cop who brought him in was saying:

" . . . no identification, but clothes look expensive . . . booze . . . kept asking for you . . . sorry about . . ."

"It's all right," Delancy said. "Leave us alone, okay?"

The uniformed cop looked relieved to do just that. Delancy took a chair from across the room and moved it to face the one Madden sat in. He straddled it, his stomach facing the backrest, his forearms on the top of the chair.

"How do you feel, Joe?"

"Like hell." It couldn't have been truer. "And I guess I look that way, too."

Delancy looked at the stitching on Madden's face. It ran from just under the middle of the left eye downward in a jagged line which ended an inch or so to the left and just under the lower lip. "I've seen worse," he said. "Want to tell me what happened?"

"I told them all I know," Madden said. "I was drunk and tired and . . . I shouldn't have been out. That's what they said, Sergeant, they said I shouldn't have been out. But I had to . . . I just couldn't stay in that apartment . . . "

"It's Leo, Joe. And I understand."

"I thought maybe you might."

"You didn't get a look at him? Were there more than one?"

"I don't know, I only remember the one, and I didn't get a look at him not a good one."

"White or black?"

"I don't know."

"Well, if you don't know that—"

"No use looking at the book, right?"

Delancy nodded. "What did he get? Your wallet, I guess, since I'm told you had no identification. What else?"

"I don't know about the wallet. I don't think I was carrying it. But—"

He had been holding everything in check, waiting for Delancy, and now that the big cop was here, he felt it give way—all of it. His head pounded with a fury he'd never felt before, his insides felt as if they'd been walked on with spiked boots, but he didn't care.

"My watch," he said. "They got that. And—" It came out in a sob which racked his entire body ". . . my wedding ring. *They took my wedding ring, the bastards!*"

He felt the cop's big hands grip his heaving shoulders. Delancy waited until the heaving stopped.

"We'll take a description of the ring and the watch. If they're pawned—"

"Goddamn it! They kill her, then they—"

But he couldn't get the rest of it out. His throat constricted with a desperate attempt of his insides to purify themselves, but there was nothing left in him but the dry heaves. When they subsided, Delancy took his hands from Madden's shoulders and stood.

"Come on. Let's get a bandage on that face, and then I'll give you a lift home."

In the car neither man seemed in the mood for talk, but Madden knew that Delancy had something on his mind. "Go ahead," he told the cop. "Tell me that I was stupid."

"I don't have to tell you that, Joe. But there is something I should tell you. You may not think so, but you were a lucky man tonight."

Madden or a part of him, wanted to laugh, but he didn't.

"Lucky," Delancy repeated. "That knife point did a lot of damage, but it could have cost you an eye. Looks to me like you fell into it, the way the cut is so jagged."

"Lucky," Madden said in a hollow voice.

"Something else, Joe. You're lucky that wedding ring of yours was a little larger than it had to be."

76

Madden's head jerked up. "How did you—I mean, that's right, it was a little loose, but how did you—"

"Because otherwise that ring finger might have been twisted broken—or worse. Knives have other uses than slicing up faces."

When they reached the apartment, Delancy double-parked the car and walked Madden to the door. The inner door had not yet been fixed, Madden saw. It opened to Dalancy's slight push. At the elevator Delancy said, "I'll ride up with you, Joe. To make sure you can get in your place."

"I don't think I locked it. I don't remember locking it, but maybe I did. You carry a set of master keys with you?"

Delancy shook his head. He opened his wallet and produced a plastic card. "This is all the key I need, Joe—to nine-tenths of the doorlocks in this city."

"That card?"

"You're supposed to be the engineer. It's a fairly simple thing. But that's how apartments get burgled when the people who live there think everything's locked up tight."

"And how women get raped . . ."

Delancy nodded.

The apartment was unlocked when they reached the door. As Madden opened it, he turned to the policeman. "Look, I'm sorry that I—"

"It's all right, Joe. You want me to come in for a while?"

Madden said no. "I'd be lousy company right now, besides I think I'd better get some sleep." He laughed sharply. "That's why I went walking, so I could sleep. Now I think I can."

Delancy's expression was noncommunicative as he

handed Madden a business card. "Get your sleep, Joe. Then give me a call sometime tomorrow. I want the description of your watch and ring. Also by then you'll have a chance to determine whether you still have your wallet and your credit cards. Something else, Joe—when you call me tomorrow, I want you sober. I want you to stay off the booze for the next couple days, all right? No more crazy stunts like tonight."

"I hear you," Madden said quietly. "No more booze for a while."

"And—?"

"And no more crazy stunts like tonight."

When the door was closed, Madden leaned his back against it. As he heard the big cop's footfalls move down the hall toward the elevator, he grinned. The stitches hurt even through the dullness of the novocaine they had shot him with, but the hurt felt right somehow.

He had not lied to the cop. He wasn't going to touch liquor for the next few days. He had to get himself together, both physically and mentally. Because he had a plan.

It wasn't much of a plan, not yet. His brain was in no fix to put anything into shape which properly could be called a *plan,* but he had the outline for what he was going to do. *You're supposed to be the engineer,* Delancy had said. It was obvious to Madden, even in his present state, that some engineering in this city was badly needed. But the big cop was dead right about the rest, too.

No more crazy stunts like tonight.

No. The nights to come were going to be a lot different.

A hell of a lot different.

78

# SEVEN

He awoke with pain. Probably it was what finally caused him to wake in the first place, the pain which flamed through the left side of his face. He felt that pain acutely. He felt other aches in both his head and body. He also felt hungry.

The sun streamed through the window, its beams highlighting the digital clock beside his bed. It was one in the afternoon. No wonder he was starved. He'd had nothing to eat since the burgers Delancy had brought the previous day—and whatever remnants of that which had been left in his stomach had long since been discharged, either on the dark street or in the emergency room.

He sat up in the bed and looked at the heap of clothing which lay at its foot. Two piles of clothing actually, both with their share of his insides staining them, one pile carrying his blood. It was like the war all over again . . .

And he needed a shave badly. His fingers touched the left side of his face. It would be a while before he'd be able to shave that mess thoroughly, but he'd do the best he could.

He stood now, naked, beside the bed, wondering what he should do first. A man has to have a plan, even in the most mundane of things. *You're the engineer,* he told himself. Very well.

Breakfast was his first need.

The coffee from yesterday, which Delancy had made, was still in the pot. He took out the innards of the percolator and plugged in the cord to let it come to a boil. It would be stale, yes, but the hell with it. If it was all that bad, he could make a fresh pot. In the meantime . . .

It had been a while since he'd fried his own bacon, and the snapping and crackling of the strips in the black iron frying pan sounded good to his ears. The smell of the burning fat, that too felt good in his nostrils, a clean substitute to the smell of whiskey and his own vomit which seemed to have taken a permanent hold in the inner reaches of his nose.

He had planned to fry eggs with the bacon grease, eggs to accompany the bacon, but no sooner were the strips of pork dried out on a paper towel than he wolfed them down. The taste was something out of this world, as if he'd tasted nothing like it before. He'd overdone some of the strips, others were not done well enough, but nonetheless all of it was good.

He considered the problem of the eggs as he poured himself a cup of steaming coffee. He still felt hungry and knew that he had every right in the world to feel hungry. His tastebuds were screaming for more, even as the hot black coffee scalded them to screams from a different cause.

Madden smiled. It pained his face to smile, but he held the expression. He didn't have to decide now whether or not breakfast—or breakfast-lunch as it would be—was over yet. He would wait, until after he had that shave.

Back in the bathroom now, he took off the bandage

and looked closely at his face. The jagged line with its nylon crosshatchings was ugly, there was no doubt about it. But somehow the look pleased him. It gave his face a quality it had never had before, the quality of ferocity, of cruelty, of ruthlessness. Not the most human of qualities, to be sure, but then that was as it should be. Because he, Joe Madden, was no longer the most human of men. He had accepted their rules.

Them. The animals.

They were ruthless. They were cruel. They operated outside the laws of men.

And now they had another convert. But from an unexpected quarter.

One of the helpless prey—one of the square and civilized victims—had joined them in their disdain for the rules of civilization. He, Joe Madden, was now joining them in their jungle warfare. But there was a difference—no, two differences.

One, he was seeking *them* out.

Two, he was smarter than they were.

Now, that shave, No—first a shower, a thorough cleansing shower, and a shampoo to cleanse the top of his head so that maybe the brain beneath it could think more clearly . . .

It was ten minutes before two when he was ready to shave. He felt clean as never before in his life; now all that remained was to clean the hair from his face—as much as he could.

He took delight, as always, from the cleansing, even smiling painfully at the area of the wound, at the stubble of growth there which he knew would get darker and longer each day. *They brought it on themselves,* he thought; then he wondered exactly what he meant by that. He thought about it while cleaning the razor, but could come to no definitive answer. None-theless, it was right. The thought was very right, he decided.

Then a full look at himself—in the mirror behind the bedroom door. Not very encouraging. That extra fat around the middle . . .

Two days ago—it seemed centuries ago—he had looked at himself and felt good. Now . . .

The gut was soft, so were the chest and shoulder muscles. Too soft. Well, that could be remedied, given time. Eat right, exercise properly . . .

He inhaled, filling his lungs with air, then pushed out a fist toward his mirror image. The hand-to-hand combat scream was silent, but the air blasted outward and the stitches on his face shrieked from the effort.

Not good enough. Not half good enough. There were karate classes in this city. Should he—

No. There wasn't time enough. The work had to begin long before he could be all that proficient at one of the martial arts. His combat training of more than twenty years ago would have to suffice. He could toughen his body, increase his skills, but these would be slow processes. He would use what he had to, he decided, to better enable him to do the work he had set for himself, but in the meantime the work had to begin . . .

The work.

That was how he thought of it now. The work, the job he had demanded from himself. That's what it was. *You're supposed to be the engineer.* And so he was, but what is an engineer? A person who creates some kind of system, something that functions in a way which is important to the continuance of civilization. But they—

Them . . .

They worked to destroy civilization, the rules, the laws, the fabric of organized life itself. *They* were of the jungle, he of the organized society.

But organized society—

Delancy had said it all. The undermanned police force, the crowded courts, all of it—

Organized society obviously considered itself above dealing with the jungle. And now that he thought about it, just how many dwellers in the organized world knew about the jungle which surrounded them?

Quite a few.

Madden, like any New Yorker, read the papers. Hell, that was part of being one of the civilized. You read the papers. But there on those pages—not those which told the stock market quotations nor the ones which tattled on who's who in the eyes of the big city gossips nor in the space devoted to the various arts of civilized man, but on earlier pages—it was all there. The brutal stabbing of some poor girl who cried for help. The just-as-brutal turning of the head of some passerby.

Involvement. A key word for an engineer, or at least an engineer who thought like Joe Madden. If you didn't *involve* yourself completely in what the client was trying to do—or thought he wanted to try to do; and there was a difference!—then you were just an onlooker. And old man Chilton had said it enough times:

"You want to be an on-looker? Then perhaps you should remain at home watching daytime TV."

He'd never said that to Joe Madden, but he'd said it to some of those young engineers who applied for work with Chilton and Harris.

And the old man was right.

No, Madden did not believe—as did many engineers—that it was the skill they shared which could suddenly transform society into something greater than it was or greater than it ever had been. The old man himself didn't believe that. But Madden did agree with the old man on one point. Man had created his own ability to engineer his society's future. Having done so, it was his duty to do what he could to bring about a future which was deemed desirable—not by just the professional engineer alone, but by the philosophers, the theologians, and the commonest of working people.

"Joe Madden," he now said aloud to his reflection in the mirror. "Joe Madden—engineer."

No sooner had he heard the last word when he dropped to the floor laughing. He knocked out eleven push-ups, then he fell all the way to the floor. It will improve, he thought to himself. He stood, looking in the mirror for calories dropped during the short exercise session. He laughed again. There was no improvement. He laughed not so much at that observation as at his ability to agree that the observation had been correct. He was his own client in this matter—and clients have a way with wishful thinking. He wasn't going to make that mistake—neither as client nor as advisor.

"I'm hungry," he said aloud.

"You're also fat," he answered himself.

He laughed again. "Fine. We've had breakfast. Now let's have lunch—to celebrate."

His mind supplied the response: Celebrate—that you're fat?

"No," he told his mirror image. "To celebrate that I'm hungry!"

He ate three eggs plus another four strips of bacon, plus a tomato with thick gobs of mayonnaise. He drank four cups of coffee black, then he drank a full can of V-8 juice—without the usual complement of gin or vodka; only salt and pepper and a lethal dose of tabasco sauce was added.

Then he took another shower.

He was toweling himself off when the telephone rang. He purposely took the call on the bedroom phone, so that he could see the time. The time was three ten.

The voice was Delancy's.

"How are you, Joe?"

"Fine. How are you?"

A pause. "You been—ah, drinking?"

"Coffee and V-8. It's not the same as tomato juice but—"

"I've heard the ads, Joe. I asked you how you felt."

"Considering . . . fine."

"I told you I'd be wanting a description of the ring and watch."

"Fine. I can do better than that. A picture."

Delancy repeated the last word.

"Sure," Madden said. "If you don't mind me being in there with them. I figure, what with all the scientific equipment you've got, you won't have much trouble enlarging the photo. If necessary, I can give your people the necessary instructions—"

The cop broke in. "I don't much like your tone, Joe."

"Then you can—"

He stopped. No, this didn't make sense. Not only was the man on the other end of the line somebody who had gone out of his way to help him, but he was *the law*. Careful, Joe Madden, be very careful.

"Sorry," he said.

It was the right thing to have said.

"Look, Joe—if you're still—"

"No—Leo," the name of the man sounded funny to his own ears. But it was what the cop wanted, he was sure of it. "Look, Leo, it's not your fault. Christ, how could it be? But I do think a photograph of the ring and the watch would be better than any verbal description, right?"

"Right. When can I come over and—"

"Now, if you like. But I'd rather you didn't."

"Why's that?"

"I need my sleep. My beauty rest."

"Tonight?"

"Sure," Madden said. "Any time after seven."

And as he hung up, he grinned. There it was. Sometime after seven there would be a policeman in his home. He'd talk to that policeman, give him a color print of a photograph taken on the island of Aruba which showed off his ring and watch—both new—and then the policeman would be gone.

And then Joe Madden would be gone.

Out to do his work.


The last of the coffee pot was drained and Madden considered brewing another. He decided against it. It was almost four fifteen now. He had less than three hours before Delancy showed up, and there was a lot to be done between then and now.

He was going to get one of them tonight.

He was going to get one of them good—and permanent.

There was another full can of V-8 in the cupboard. It was—had been—their standard mix for Bloody Marys, but he had no urge to mess around with liquor now. No, Delancy was right, righter than even the cop himself knew. A clear head. He'd need it.

After all, how long had it been?

How long had it been—since he'd killed somebody?

And that had been with a gun, a rifle. A long-distance weapon that dropped the man you'd killed before you had a chance to see his face. Now, tonight, there was no gun.

But what was there?

That was the question, and it was a question he had to answer in the next three hours. Because, as soon as Delancy left his apartment, somebody else was leaving. And that somebody else was going to be armed to kill.

Armed how?

He stood now, still naked, in the kitchen. He realized that there was an abundance of weaponry—in the drawer just to the right of the sink.

That was where Sara had kept her knives.

He cleared the counter of the dishes and the debris of his breakfast and lunch and swabbed it down with the sponge he took from on top of the sink. The sponge was red-pink. Appropriate, he thought to himself, even though the proper shade of red wasn't there. He dried the countertop with a paper towel, then he opened the drawer.

For a moment he did nothing. His eyes locked onto the array of blades within the drawer. Then, his face grim, he began the selection process.

It took him a total of ten minutes to make the final selection. There had been four contenders.

The first was a small meat cleaver. As he handled it, he thought of the old Tong wars on the west coast. The weapon—or something similar to it—had worked well enough then; why not now? Three reasons, he decided. The cleaver, though not all that large, was large enough to make concealment a problem. That was the first problem with it. The second was the difficulty in getting it out swiftly for action. The L-shape easily could stick in his pocket, leaving him a victim to another's weapon while he worked like hell at tearing up the lining of his coat. The third problem was the utility of the thing once he'd gotten it out. The cutting edge was sharp enough, and easily could kill with one blow, but the problem was that there only was one kind of blow he could deliver with effectiveness—a chopping motion, whether vertical or horizontal or diagonal.

No. He wanted something with more versatility, something with which he could slash and thrust.

The cleaver went back into the drawer.

Next for consideration came a wooden-handled Hoffritz carving knife. It was the longest knife in the drawer, measuring almost fourteen inches from end to end. The point of the thing was prick-finger sharp, and a couple of runs through Sara's electric knife sharpener and the rest of it would slice a dropped hair. But Madden didn't like it. For one thing, the blade curved upward, so that its point was higher than the top edge of the handle. To thrust it outward, his wrist would have to be bent back too far. He tried it four times and felt the awkward strain. There was also the thinness of the blade which bothered him. No, the thing wasn't sturdy enough.

It joined the cleaver in the drawer.

He next considered a second carving knife, this one, as the Hoffritz, made in Germany, but unlike the other, steel from end to end. Twelve and a quarter inches it measured, its blade less wide—for easier entry, he thought. But the grip was thin as well, and the blade again too pliable. If it struck a bone it might deflect— or halt . . .

No. It was a good-looking thing, designed in a very clean modern style, but no. Fine for carving a turkey, maybe, but he had other and more active victims in mind.

Its delivery into the drawer was accompanied by the bell-like ring of steel against steel.

There were two more candidates.

But they really was no contest between the two.

The bone-handled steak knife felt good to the touch, its curved-down handle fitting nicely into Madden's hand. But the point of the blade was rounded, no good at all for thrusting, and the blade bottom was serrated and not sharp. In addition, the end-to-end measurement of the knife was but nine and a half inches at most.

There was only one left. And that it should be the one made Madden's mouth turn upward into a cruel grin.

It measured almost exactly twelve inches, more than seven and a quarter inches of blade. The steel was deep—measuring one and a half inches in depth at the hilt. The butcher knife's point was sharp to the touch and located well below the top of the wooden handle. And the blade itself was thick enough so that he hardly could move it from side to side with full finger pressure.

It felt good in his hand, this butcher knife did, but there was another reason why this should be his weapon. It was a reason which made everything right.

He held the blade up so that he could read the writing:

R. H. Forchner Co. And to the right of that a bird —a dove? If so, that too was ironic—with some kind of branch or flower in its mouth. Maybe the olive branch! If so, the symbol was sadly out of place.

Made in Switzerland, stainless steel.

Switzerland, home of the negotiators. Again, why not? The blade would be doing its share of negotiating—in the only terms the animals recognized.

Stainless steel. Now, maybe. But later—later tonight—there would be a few stains.

Yes, this was the one. Right length, right thickness, right grip, right words on its blade. And something else.

He knew. He didn't poke around Sara's kitchen much, but this much he knew:

If Sara had had a favorite knife, this one was it.

Her own favorite blade, then, would avenge—

He stopped his thoughts. He held the edge of the blade up to the light. Sara's favorite knife, yes, but she hadn't taken all that good care of it. There were six nicks in the edge, four of them quite deep, but none of them too deep they couldn't be repaired.

Within ten minutes he had the edge he wanted. After the electric sharpener had completed its work on the main cutting edge, Madden had inserted the top portion of the point, grinding down that edge to about an inch but careful not to grind too far. The last thing he wanted was the point so thin that it might snap on contact with something more substantial than what was the intended target.

The weapon in his right fist, he strode into the bedroom. Facing the full length mirror there, he spread his legs and allowed his arms to fall by his side in a rest position. Then, as if on some kind of signal, he snapped the blade upward.

He grinned dryly at the mirror image as he imagined the stark terror the sudden sight of that blade would

C'mon

**Come for the filter.** **You'll stay for the taste.**

KENT

WITH
THE FAMOUS MICRONITE FILTER

KING SIZE

KING SIZE

KENT

WITH
THE FAMOUS MICRONITE FILTER

Warning: The Surgeon General Has Determined That Cigarette Smoking Is Dangerous to Your Health.

16 mg. "tar," 1.0 mg. nicotine av. per cigarette, FTC Report Apr. '75.

# Newport

## *Alive with pleasure!*

Newport

20 CLASS A CIGARETTES

**Newport**

MENTHOL KINGS

17 mg. "tar", 1.2 mg. nicotine, av. per cigarette, FTC Report Apr. '75.

cause in his victim's eyes—eyes that would bulge like bloated bubbles about to pop before the top and shaft of Madden's knife would slice through vocal cords and gullet.

He whipped the blade back downward, then again snapped it forward, this time at chest level, this time his right foot stepping in with the thrust. He imagined the cry of the invisible man on the other end of that thrust.

Again he grinned.

Then he frowned.

It was wrong, the way he was imagining his attack. Yes, he should practice and he should get used to how the weapon felt in his hand as he moved it toward the target, but he was going about things wrongly. Handling the end-game of thrust and slash was one thing, but that depended a lot on the beginning—how he would draw the blade from his person to get it out for its proper business.

He placed the knife down on the top of the still unmade bed, keeping his eyes on it for most of the time it took him to dress. He dressed fully, with clean, fresh smelling clothes. Trousers, shirt, tie, socks, shoes, suit jacket—and then his lined raincoat. When that was completed, he again faced the mirror, knife in hand. Now the important question:

Where to hide the knife?

He had thought it was going to be another drawn-out process of elimination, such as that involved in his selection of the weapon, but he was wrong. His mirror image told him immediately the proper place. Up the left sleeve of his jacket. He lay the blade on top of his forearm, still holding the handle, then he drew it forward slowly in as fluid a motion as possible. Perfect.

Again he tried it, this time less slowly. Again perfect. Fine. He could practice his "quick draw" later, after he'd solved the next problem—a sheath of some kind for the weapon.

That he needed one was obvious. He couldn't walk around holding the thing in by the handle, and he'd need some self-protection, to insure that the newly sharpened, double-edged point of the blade didn't slice into his inner elbow.

But what? What was the best kind of sheath?

He sat on the edge of the bed and thought about it. No sooner did he do so when he felt unusually warm. Of course. The raincoat. He stood and took it off, also ridding himself of the suit jacket. He looked down at his forearm. Whatever he used, the sheath would have to be fastened to his arm at two points, one near the wrist, the other nearer the elbow. Shouldn't be too difficult a problem. After all, he was an engineer, wasn't he?

He no sooner asked the question of himself when he had the answer. He remembered when Sara had brought a set of new steak knives home. They had come wrapped in special sheaths—of soft cardboard. His sheath wouldn't be all that soft, however.

He was completely outfitted in less than fifteen minutes.

The sheath itself was nothing more than a simple sleeve, formed from the cardboard backing of an eight and a half by eleven lined tablet. The cardboard had been cut to the precise shape of the knife blade, which Madden had carefully traced around with ballpoint pen, being sure to leave about a quarter of an inch all around. Then he cut out the resultant long triangular shape, carefully folding it down the center. Next came the tape—heavy masking tape, four applications of it—to completely fasten the two flaps together. He tried the knife. It fit perfectly. What's more, it came out easily—but not *too* easily. The last step was to fasten it under his forearm. Easy again, because of the tape. Five full winds in two places, right over his striped shirt.

He stood now again before the mirror, again with his suit jacket and raincoat on. The butt of the knife handle was protruding just enough. He stared at himself. This was the crucial test. Crucial—

But he laughed in spite of himself.

He felt like Matt Dillon. Like that opening scene on the main street of Dodge City.

Draw!

He drew.

It was clumsy the first time. The second time was better. On the third try, he thought he'd beaten even Matt Dillon's time. He could almost hear the "Gunsmoke" theme music.

He set the knife down on the top of the bed, then he took off his coat and jacket. Very carefully he stripped off the two tape-bonds from his shirt. His watch said it was close to quarter of six. He looked around the room. Sloppy, very sloppy. It wouldn't do.

Nothing about him could be sloppy tonight. Nothing at all.

It was while he was searching for the photograph that Delancy was coming for that he found another.

Sara.

Beautiful Sara, standing in the lobby of their hotel on the island of Aruba, the place of their honeymoon. Quiet, nothing-to-do Aruba. But they hadn't cared. That was in fact what had made them choose the island. Nothing but the sun and the sand and each other.

He stared at the photograph.

I can't bring that night back. I can't bring you back.

But I'll make them pay, baby. I swear it—*I'll make them pay!*

# EIGHT

"You look better," Delancy said, sitting down on the couch. "I see you did a little bit of cleaning up, too."

Madden nodded. "What do you drink Leo? You look like a Scotch man."

"I am."

"Sorry. I went through all of that yesterday."

"Just as well. I'm on duty."

"Coffee? None's made, but I can—"

"No. I drink so much of the goddamned stuff. I think that's all that's going through my veins." He looked at Madden. "What are *you* having?"

"Tomato juice. There was a can of it I found earlier back in the cupboard. I ran out of V-8."

"Mixing anything with it?"

"I will, maybe. Maybe when my head starts feeling right, when I'm used to things—when I've got something to celebrate."

Their eyes locked and held for a good ten seconds. It was Delancy who looked away first. "If you're pouring some tomato juice, I see no reason why I shouldn't join you."

Before Madden went to the kitchen he gave the policeman the photograph which showed both ring and watch. When he returned, the photo was nowhere in sight. Probably in one of the pockets of Delancy's overcoat which, Madden now noticed, the big man had not bothered to remove. Good. That meant he wasn't planning on staying long.

But as he sipped from the glass Madden had handed him, he didn't look in all that much of a rush to move, either.

"Tell me, Joe . . . in looking for this picture . . . you obviously had to look at others, right?"

There was something in the way he said it that made Madden wary. "Why do you ask, Leo?"

"Never mind. I asked. You going to answer?"

He sat in the chair across from the couch. "Okay, I'll answer. Sure—I looked at several pictures."

"Of Sara and you—and of Sara alone."

"That's right. We don't take—*didn't* take—pictures of strangers." He allowed a mouthful of tomato juice to sit in his mouth for the count of five before he swallowed it. "But you've got a reason for asking me, right?"

Delancy pursed his thick lips. "Like I said, Joe, you *look* good. I'm trying to find out how you *feel*."

Madden's voice grew hard. "You don't notice any champagne corks popping, do you?"

"Joe—"

"Leo, let me ask you something. You told me earlier that there's only a snowball's chance in hell that the filth who killed my wife are going to get caught—you told me that, right?"

"I told you that, yes." Quietly, he said it.

Quietly, Madden came back. "And what about your woman?"

"She was a girl, Joe. She wasn't even really a full-grown woman yet. I—" He stopped, his eyes falling to the glass he now held with both hands. "She was beautiful, Joe."

"Sara was beautiful, Leo."

Delancy looked up at him, his facial lines hardening. "That's right, it's your wife's death which brings me here, isn't it?"

Madden suddenly felt sorry—for himself, but even more for the big cop. After all, Madden had adjusted— or thought he had. But Delancy . . .

"Leo, tell me. No, don't tell me, not if you don't want to, but—"

"Ask it, Joe. We're on the subject, so you might as well."

"Never mind."

*"Ask it!"*

The words came out as two gunshots in the apartment, the man's eyes suddenly fierce on Madden's.

"All right, I'll ask. But there are two questions, not one. The first, I think I already know the answer to, but I'll ask. Did they get caught, Leo? The ones who took out—"

He couldn't remember the name. Delancy supplied it quietly:

"Margaret."

"Margaret," Madden repeated. "Did they—or him, whoever—did justice get them?"

It took the cop a while before replying. "He . . . I think of him as just one, Joe . . . I hope he's gotten his."

"But you don't know."

"No. I don't know. I know he never came to his just end for the crime against Margaret, but these people— they're habitual offenders. I hope—and like to think— that he got what he deserved for some other—"

"But not for Margaret," Madden prodded.

He had prodded just a bit too much.

Delancy shot to his feet. "What the hell are you saying, Madden?"

"I thought it was Joe. Joe and Leo, old buddies in war—old buddies who were bonded together because they lost the war and lost it in a similar way—"

"What's this about a war?"

Madden now rose. "You don't think there is a war going on? You—you who has to face it every day? You—you've got to look at Joe Madden now. How many Joe Maddens have you looked at, *Sergeant?* What the goddamned hell does it take for you to see that—"

And then he halted. He'd gone too far, and he knew it for a fact, "Okay. I'm sorry."

"Don't apologize, Joe. There's no sense to it."

Madden half smiled. "I agree. We're not the enemy, are we? It's those others—the animals."

"Animals," Delancy repeated. "Why do you call them that?"

"Because that's what they are. They're not humans, Leo. They couldn't be! Humans don't do what those bastards did to Sara, to your—"

"No, Joe, you're wrong. Humans kill like no other animals do—for the pleasure of it sometimes. It happens, I know. But the jungle animal only kills to—"

"To what? Survive? That's what they say about the filth that killed my Sara! They must kill, they have to—they don't want to, maybe, but they need the money she's got in her purse, maybe her TV set or silver. No, Leo, they're animals."

Madden quieted himself. "The second question, Leo. You said you'd answer it."

"And I will."

"How does it feel when—when you kill one of them?"

Delancy's face didn't react one way or the other. It was the same stone face he'd been wearing for the last three or four minutes. "I don't ... quite follow you, Joe."

"Yes you do, Leo. You carry a gun, right?"

Delancy nodded slowly.

"All right. You've used it, also right?"

"Joe—"

"I thought you'd level with me."

"Okay. I've used it."

"*Killed* with it?"

A whisper: "Yes."

"I'm not sure I heard you, Leo."

"*Yes.*"

Madden stopped. And waited as Delancy's heaving tion, Leo—did you enjoy the killing? Did you, when you were pulling that trigger, think that maybe—and maybe hope—that it was *him*? How did you feel when you saw him fall, his blood spattering the pavement, his eyes bulging out at you in horror, his—"

"Joe—for Christ's sake—*stop it!*"

Madden stopped. And waited as Delancy's heaving chest quieted.

"Joe, it's not like that, it really isn't."

"I'm not the police commissioner, Leo. You don't have to lie to me. I know how I feel, and I know how you must have felt. You can't tell me that you—"

"All right, Joe. In the beginning, yes, there was the kind of feeling you're talking about. But I got over it."

Madden smiled. "No, Leo, I don't think you did. I don't think you got over it at all. Do you want to know why? I'll tell you anyway. You haven't gotten over *it* because you've never gotten over *her*."

His smile faded. He was more sincere now than he had been all night, maybe than he'd been in years. "Leo, she must have been some girl. She really must have been."

"She was, Joe."

He stood there, this cop who had never married, this man who other men might look at disparagingly because he was fat and bald and dressed sloppily. Joe Madden looked at him with a feeling of kinship, a feeling of sharing. The same look was reflected in the other man's eyes.

"Joe..."

Madden tried to smile, but it didn't come off. Delancy went on:

"Look, my girl and your wife—they were two good women. We've lost them. The city, the world has lost them, but you and me—we feel it the most. We've just got to ... adjust."

"You've adjusted?"

A pause. "Better than you, I think. Like I said when I first saw you tonight, Joe, you look good. Real good. Too good. Whatever thoughts you got going through that head of yours ..."

"You don't approve of them."

"I don't know what they are. I don't want to know."

It was a gamble, and Madden took it:

"Which means, Sergeant, that you *do* know. You know what I've been thinking."

Delancy appeared not even to hear the statement. He was all the way to the door when he turned and replied to it.

"Joe, none of us was brought up to be a killer. I

know, that's the problem—as you see it. You look at it and ask how the decent law-abiding man is to protect himself. You've got a right to ask that. The official answer is that the law provides for your protection."

"The official answer—" Madden began.

"Is bullshit," the cop completed. "But it's nonetheless official. A citizen cannot take the law into his own hands."

Madden nodded agreement. This juncture was no point for him to argue. But he couldn't help making one pertinent comment, the first part of which was a question.

"Leo, let me ask you one more. The scum out there that kills, they're not all that high on the IQ scale, right? I mean, if you had to rate them against the average population—"

"They'd come out on the stupid side, yes."

Madden could not help but grin. He didn't want to, in fact he desperately *tried* not to, but it came out nonetheless.

"Well then, it seems to me that a smart avenger— well, if your *stupids* get off more than fifty percent of the time—"

"Good night, Joe," Delancy said.

"Good night, Leo," Madden said back. But even before he'd pronounced the second syllable of the big cop's name, the door was closed. With Sergeant Leo Delancy on the other side.

To be sure, the policeman's departure was abrupt, but Madden didn't care all that much. His watch told him that the time was ten minutes before eight. His nostrils flared.

Already he could taste the cold air of the outside night.

The night of the jungle—the jungle full of the savage animals.

The beasts it was his task to hunt.

He could feel it now. They were assembling out there, moving into their dark corners and waiting for their prey. He visualized the long shape of Manhattan Island, and yes, there they all were—in the darkest of recesses. East Side, West Side, all around the town.

In front of his mirror now, his suit jacket and lined raincoat on, the knife in its sheath retaped under his left forearm, he looked at his reflection in the mirror.

"East Side, West Side, all around the town," he said aloud.

He'd never had much of a singing voice, but tonight the sound of it was as if he were a stage actor. He thought about that, he spoke to his mirror image about it:

"If I be an actor," he said in a mock British-Shakespearean accent, "then let it be an actor in a tragedy."

But his mirrored eyes caught his own, and the humor died.

The tragedy has happened already, was the message the mirror sent to him.

He accepted it for what it was worth, buttoning up the raincoat as he did. He knew he had to make some sort of vocal response—he had to. Otherwise he could not leave his mirror image. He knew what he was going out this night to do, and so did that look-alike figure in the mirror. Therefore, they both had to agree that it was right. He knew what he wanted to say—in thought, but not the precise words. And they had to be exactly, precisely right. After all, he was an engineer . . .

Even though that fierce look-alike in the mirror had addressed him as an actor or playwright.

*The tragedy had happened already . . .*

"Bullshit!" he roared at the mirror. And he grinned, so widely that the strain on the stitches made him think they were going to pop, but he didn't care.

"Bullshit!" he said again. "All full plays—even tragedies—have three acts!"

He didn't say the rest. He didn't have to, because he was certain that even the mirror image understood.

A tragedy it might be, but only the first act had been played. That left two more.

And Joe Madden was going to make sure those following acts—and each of their scenes—were as bloody as the first. He took off the coat and jacket and made himself two thick sandwiches of luncheon meat, cheese, and lettuce. With them he had two cups of coffee. The meal was satisfying and he enjoyed it at his leisure. Then coat and jacket were back on and he was once again before the mirror, practicing.

It was not quite nine o'clock when he left the apartment.

# *NINE*

He walked east, just as he had walked the previous night, the lights and sounds of First Avenue not bothersome to him at all tonight. The night was cold, but his head was clear and his stomach warm from his supper meal. Just before he'd left the apartment, he'd considered a short drink, but the consideration was brief. No, tonight he wanted his mind to be at its best, his reflexes at their quickest. The whiskey might have been useful to give him a bit more nerve, it was true, but he didn't need it. What's more he didn't want false courage. If he didn't have the real guts to do what he wanted to do, then let it remain undone. Also he wanted the complete responsibility for his acts to be his own; there would be no opportunity for him to blame everything on alcohol thoughts.

He crossed First, then turned to look at the traffic on the street. Two couples were piling out of a taxi, laughing at some joke or other. They were in their late thirties, the men were, the women about ten years younger. Madden knew the signs. Two men who should have been on commuter trains hours ago and two secretary types whose social lives revolved around short affairs with married men. Too bad. The women were not that unattractive. Anywhere else but New York—or maybe it was any big city, but especially New York—they'd have a chance at meeting potential marriage material. But here, the men they met in their daily work-world already wore gold or silver rings, already had their quota of two kids, house, car, and a lawn to putter around on weekends. There always was the hope, of course, that the girl plus the aura of a wild city life-style would attract the man to the extent that he'd give up his suburban life, and divorce was a lot easier these days . . .

What was he doing? Standing on a corner, philosophizing about these people and their problems, when he had his own work to do, and when they didn't seem to have any problems at all. True, their laughs seemed a little forced, but regardless of what problems they thought they had, their problems were minor. They were, even to their own way of thinking, in a gain position. He was in a loss position.

Enough of this crap. It was time to begin evening the score.

He continued along Seventy-seventh, heading east. It was odd, he remembered going this way the previous night, remembered something about wanting to be near the water. He didn't know why he was walking the same path tonight, but it somehow seemed right. Maybe he'd get lucky. Maybe the one who slashed him last night would be out on the streets again, and just maybe he'd try his luck again. The problem was finding the exact same place. It never had occurred to him to ask any of the police just where it was he was found. That was stupid; he should have—

No, it was better he didn't know. In fact—

At York he deliberately turned north. He was certain he'd crossed the street here the previous night and had continued east, but not tonight. If by chance he did find the same place and if by chance he found his man—any of his men—there, the killing would look like too much of a coincidence. Besides, the odds against his finding *the* one were in no way possible. And it wasn't important, anyway.

He was at war with them, *all* of them. There was nothing in the way of the symbolic to be attached to the first of the enemy to be met in the field. He was to be number one, that was his only significance.

The wooden handle of the knife felt cold where it butted up against the inside of Madden's wrist.

He crossed to the east side of York at Seventy-ninth. At Eightieth he again turned eastward. The houses on both sides of the street might have been splendid old structures, brand new moderns or run-down tenements. They didn't register now. All that registered were the patches of darkness, the shadows out of which, sooner or later, one of *them* would be coming . . .

As his eyes concentrated on the dark places, his ears too had eliminated sounds which were not germaine to his quest. The noises of traffic, of people moving within the houses, he didn't hear, but small sounds—like that of a garbage can cover shifting, probably due to the hunger-mission of some stray cat—those he accepted, sorted out, and where he could, identified.

At East End Avenue he turned north again. At the corner of Eighty-second the hair to the back of his neck tingled. He was being watched, he could feel it.

The man was leaning against the corner. He was black and wore a leather coat which, although not that out of date in style, had seen better days. Madden stopped and looked directly at him, his eyes hardening, his right hand moving inches closer to his left wrist. They stood there, the two of them, looking at each other from a distance of at most twenty feet, for what seemed to Madden to be an eternity but probably only was a matter of seconds.

Then Madden knew it was wrong, that he was wrong. The light here was too bright. Even though the street itself seemed deserted, this didn't seem the right place. No, correct that. There was no such thing as a wrong place, was there? The daylight purse snatcher he'd seen just days ago when he and Sara . . .

His right fingertips were touching the wooden knife handle when the black man spoke:

"Hey, man . . ."

Madden waited. The black man pushed away from the corner and took two steps toward him. Madden could feel his heart pick up its beating. He took a long inhale of the cold air.

"Something you want from me?" he asked.

"A dollar, maybe?" the black man asked. "I ain't had nothing to eat all day. I got no way of getting home—up North—and my family's waiting for me. I been out looking for work all day and—"

He'd taken another two steps but now his forward movement stopped abruptly with his speech.

His eyes were flickering over Madden's face.

Over his taut mouth, and to the left side of that mouth.

"Hey man—I ain't looking for trouble or nothing . . ."

Madden's face remained hard. "But that's what you've got, *man*. Nothing."

He turned and crossed the street. As he did so, his right hand remained close to his left, his ears straining to hear any sound at all from behind him, a sound like that of leather moving on cement. But no sound came.

107

Still, it was wise to check. Some five paces onto the sidewalk, Madden turned toward the corner he'd just left.

The black man still stood where he was, shaking his head slowly.

He knew!

Some instinct, something within the man had told him that Madden was dangerous, that he was nobody to mess with. Probably the man had no intention of doing anything other than begging, but if he had—

He wouldn't have gone through with it.

Madden shrugged and continued north. Then he realized it.

Even if that black man had intentions of mugging him—

*He wouldn't have gone through with it!*

And Madden himself was to blame. He'd looked too hard-to-take, he looked as if he'd been waiting for the move—any move—which might appear threatening. He wondered—

What if, tonight, he was as he had been last night? What if he had reached that corner and that black man and hadn't been able to stare back? What would have happened then?

Maybe nothing.

Maybe—but he had no way of knowing, not now. No, last night he had been the perfect set-up. Just now, he might have put up a fight. They—the animals—would avoid somebody like that. They—the animals—preferred women or drunks, anybody who appeared to be a little helpless.

And he had looked anything but helpless. It was an error he'd not commit again. And, as he continued up East End Avenue, there was a sudden slowing of his pace, a shuffling kind of movement it was now. The movement of somebody who'd had just a little too much to drink, a man whose head might be hurting or swimming because he held it forward so, his jaw against his chest relieving the neck from the bothersome weight. He was not staggering, not quite that, but the next thing to it.

He was the fly going into the spider's parlor, a fly who wouldn't be at all able to defend himself. That's what they were to think. Until that moment of truth when they found out that the fly was in reality the spider, and that they had been sucked in, not him.

The darkness of Carl Shurz Park appealed to him. North from where he entered, he knew, was the residence of the Mayor of New York, but down here— it was a park, after all. Maybe not as dangerous as Central Park, but it would do. Off to his far right he could hear the traffic on the FDR Drive. People going north, going south, people going home and people going to work, people who were happy, people who were sad. People who had lived their lives in this jungle and who were afraid of it. Not in their automobiles and not in their locked-up homes. But how many of them ventured out on the streets at night? How many of them dared to challenge the beasts of prey who owned the city after dark?

Owned.

He thought about that. It was true, they did own the turf at night. Them, the savages who contributed nothing to the city's welfare, those who bled the honest citizens not only through their criminal acts but through their welfare handouts which showed up eventually in the big seizures from the workingman's paycheck. Taxes. *His* taxes—Madden's taxes.

He wondered now, as he staggered along in the darkness of the park, if it could possibly have happened. His tax dollars, duly paid and duly collected by the City Fathers who then duly paid out those same dollars to a "needy" family, the scions of which rode the subway at night . . .

With knives.

And on Monday night, one of those sons of bitches whose stomach was full only because of Joe Madden's tax payment—

He heard it then. Not it, them.

The footfalls behind him. More than ten yards behind him, but moving closer—closing in.

He knew it, that this time was the real thing. He didn't have to turn around to be sure, but he was very sure.

Because those footsteps had begun suddenly. They hadn't been behind him for more than those few seconds. Whoever they belonged to, he had come out from the shadows onto the walkway. He had seen Madden and had let him pass. Madden was certain of it. And then he was very certain.

"Hey, old buddy—wait up a minute!"

Madden stopped, staggering just a little. Keeping his face down into his upturned collar, he turned slowly, rocking a bit from foot to foot as if he were drunk.

It was a kid in his early twenties, by the look of him. His gnarled, light-colored hair spilled over the shoulders of the faded blue denim jacket which fit those shoulders just a bit too tightly for comfort. The trousers he wore matched, not only in their washed out color but also in the tightness of their fit. The kid was of a skinny build to begin with, but the tightness of his clothing made him look almost skeletal. And under that mess of hair, his face looked like nothing so much as a skull. The eyes were hollow, the mouth's thin lips curled up over the teeth, as if they were the death head's leer.

He stopped, just more than an arm's length from Madden.

"You talking to me?" Madden slurred.

The toothfilled grin widened further. "That's right, old buddy."

"I ain't your old buddy," Madden said, his voice even thicker now. "I don't even know you at all."

The kid laughed. "Well, let's fix that, then. Let's introduce ourselves. Let's see—you're the guy who's gonna give me all his money, and I'm the guy who's gonna take it. How's that?"

Madden screwed his face up as if what he was hearing was Greek. "That's stupid. Why would I want to do that—give you my money?"

"Because, old son—because of *this!*"

*This* was a hunting knife, still in its leather sheath as it came whipping out of the kid's back pocket. The leather slapped against the palm of the kid's left hand, the fingers of which curled around it menacingly. It was all very effective, as was the sinister laugh which followed.

"Now, let's not you and me have any trouble, okay, pal? I mean, let's don't you give me any reason to yank this blade on out of—hey!"

As if on cue, Madden's right hand whipped outward from under his left wrist. The movement was awkward—this wasn't practice now; it was for real and his hand was shaking. Not much, but too much for the smooth movement which he desired. The blade of the butcher's knife was halfway out when it seemed to catch in something. Madden took his eyes off the boy and looked down at his left sleeve. Christ! It was the bend of his own wrist halting the blade—his fingertips were pressing down on the flat of the steel!

"Hey, what—"

Correcting his wrist position, Madden yanked his knife free. His eyes now locked onto those of the kid in denim—the kid whose face registered surprise that was close to shock, so much so that he hadn't even thought to pull his own knife free from its sheath.

And now Madden laughed. "Different, isn't it?" he asked, pulling his lower face from the protection of his lapels. "Different ballgame altogether—when the mark fights back!"

The kid gasped in horror. He took a full step backward and would have taken a second. But Madden's lunge effectively had closed the distance before there was time for a second step. There was an attempt to scream—at least that's what it looked like to Madden, an instant before the first three inches of his blade went through the bastard's throat.

The wide eyes widened still further in disbelief, then the pupils rolled up into the kid's forehead, and he sagged down as if his body were so much straw, Madden's imbedded knife and hand following the downward movement. And then it seemed that there was blood everywhere—spurting from the neck of Madden's victim, covering Madden's right hand, spraying his shoes—

Quickly he yanked the blade free and stepped back as the denim-clad longhair fell over onto his face. For silent moments Madden watched as the pool of blood on the path beneath that shaggy head spread into increasing areas. Then, careful to avoid stepping into the blood, he walked around to the side of the body and bent down.

With four careful sweeps, he wiped the blade of his knife clean. Returning the weapon to its cardboard sheath, he took one last look at the first of the animals which would feel his wrath. There was something he wanted the son of a bitch to know. He wanted this filth to know why he had died. But even as Madden groped for the proper words to express it, he shook his head no and began walking the way he had come.

What the hell, proper words or improper words, the kid couldn't have heard them anyway.

At the edge of the park he cleaned the blood from his shoes in the grass, then made sure that there was none on the front of his raincoat. There was, but only on the right sleeve. His right hand, too, was sticky with the dead man's life fluid. Hand and sleeve resting deep into his right coat pocket, he hurried in the direction of home. As he came out into the lights of First Avenue, he slowed down. He had been walking too fast, so fast that he was bound to attract attention. Even now, at a slower pace, he was sure people were staring at him, that accusing eyes were narrowing toward him. But why should they be accusing? He'd just removed a menace from the city streets. Didn't they understand that? If not, shouldn't he tell them—shouldn't he shout it out to—

To whom? There were only a few people out on First Avenue at the moment, and none of them, not one, was looking at him.

It was as he turned west into Seventy-seventh that he heard the siren. It stopped him dead in his tracks. So soon? Had the remains of his handiwork been discovered all this soon? If the cops had been that fast the night he and Sara had—

But no. The shrill wail was getting louder now, much

louder. He turned around to see the white ambulance rip northward on First. An ambulance. They had sirens and so did firetrucks. He'd have to make it a point to learn the differences.

# TEN

The next morning, Friday, he awoke with a feeling that all was right with the world. The clock to the side of the bed told him it was eight thirty; the sunlight streaming through the bedroom window told him that it was a beautiful and bright morning. He had slept naked as was his usual practice, and now as he swung his legs free of the covers, the air felt good on his skin.

It wasn't until he was moving toward the bathroom that he saw it. The butcher's knife on the corner of the chest of drawers. The visual impact of the weapon stunned him for the moment.

He'd done it! He'd actually gone out and done it!

And he now felt the exhilaration which he had not felt the previous night. Last night, all he had felt was—

It was hard to say. He really didn't know what it was he felt last night. He thought that maybe what he felt was nothing at all. After the killing—directly after it— he had felt that he was being watched, but that had passed and in its stead had come the feeling that there really wasn't anybody interested enough to watch him at all. There was the sense of being alone in the great city, alone with them, the enemy. There were others, of course, the people of the city who took neither side in the war because they didn't suspect a war of this kind was going on. Those others were all around him, but they didn't count. They were nothing more than backdrop or props to the drama. They weren't the actors. No, only himself and the animals were the ones with action roles.

And this morning there was one less animal.

But last night . . .

He had felt somehow numb after the killing. Even now he could see himself, as with another eye—walking swiftly from the dead man, then slowing down so as not to appear suspicious, walking due west, then down First and turning up Seventy-seventh, and then entering his building and waiting for the elevator. Finally entering the apartment and locking the door and then pouring himself a small bourbon and carrying it into the bedroom as he peeled off his coat and jacket and then the tape from his shirt and then the rest of his clothing. He stood naked before the full length mirror, the bourbon in his hand, raising the glass in a silent toast, his eyes on the reflected eyes of the mirror surface, waiting for some kind of mental reaction.

There had been none. He drank the liquor and then went to bed where sleep claimed him immediately. A dreamless, black-void sleep.

And now this morning, the sight of the knife, and the sight of his naked form again in that mirror. But this time there was a difference in the reflection, especially around the eyes and mouth.

The lips were curled up into a half-smile, but the pale blue eyes were cold as ice. Or as death.

He had the coffee pot bubbling within minutes and went immediately to the bathroom. A cold shower, then the shave. That was his intention, but the shaving lather was no further than into the palm of his hand when he

116

realized it was no good. He couldn't shave yet; there were other things he had to do, things of more immediate concern because they were loose ends of last night's outing.

First, the raincoat. The blood still was there. At the thought, he anxiously examined his hand. There had been blood on it last night, he was certain of it. He hadn't washed last night, he also was certain of that, but this morning he hadn't been aware of anything on his fingers. True, he had showered, but—

Yes. There it was, a trace of the dried brown crust under the fingernail of his right ring finger. Carefully, with a fingernail brush, he removed it. Then another trace, minutely small between the index and middle fingers. It was odd that there wasn't more. Last night he felt as if he'd been drenched with the stuff.

It was when he picked up the raincoat from the bedroom floor and examined it closely that he knew where the blood had gone. In the right-hand pocket there was a handkerchief, stains all over it. Evidently, as he'd walked home, he'd carefully cleaned his hand. Now he had to clean the cloth.

Not the handkerchief—that was headed for a one-way trip into the incinerator shaft on his floor outside the apartment—but the coat had to be cleaned. The question was—

How do you clean bloodstains from fabric?

Sara would know, but she—

Automatically the thought cut itself off. Only a small part of it remained, the beginning. Sara would know. She would know because she had all kinds of housekeeper-helper books which had that kind of information in abundance. The thing was, which book? She could have found it, but her book storage system was something only she understood. As for him . . .

He stood now in the hall, his eyes closed. He could look directly at the several shelves—in the kitchen, living room and bedroom and the piles of books in their clothes closet—but that would take a little too much time. This way was better.

It took him a couple of seconds to clear his mind, then the kitchen bookshelves came into focus, the titles on the spines, all there for him to scan. Cookbooks of all descriptions, a *Whole Earth Catalog*, four novels, biographies of Renoir and Freud, and three paperbacks which were in the stacks backward. Next came the living room selection—nothing of interest there except a 1940-something copy of the Navy's *Bluejackets' Manual*, something Sara had bought because she wanted to know about ships' signals "in case," she said, "we ever get a boat." The fact that they'd never discussed owning a boat didn't seem to matter, but Sara was like that . . . she had been like—

He stored the *Bluejackets' Manual* as a remote possibility, then switched onto the bricks-and-boards bookshelves in the bedroom. And there he found it. *The Unhandy Handyman's Book*. He opened his eyes and went directly to the book.

Page 104 told him what he needed to know. Cold water.

It sounded simple, too simple, but the text was reassuring: *Use only cold water, and plenty of it. (Hot water sets blood stains.)* But page 104 was absolutely right. Twenty minutes later the coat was wet, but the blood was gone. Of course, there were tests the police could make which would probably find traces of the stuff within the fabric, but to make those tests they'd

118

have to have some reason. And why would anyone have a reason to test Joe Madden's coat? Only if he were caught at the scene or seen by somebody else who reported him to the police.

He laughed. If the cops were around—or if anybody was around—there wouldn't have been any action. Both Joe Madden and his victim would have seen to that.

He drank a full cup of hot coffee, then poured a second cup and brought it back into the bedroom. It was time to fix the second problem.

The knife and sheath setup.

The night before, the rig hadn't worked at all the way it was supposed to. Madden thought he knew how to correct things, but he wanted to be sure. He was. As he stood at the ready before the mirror, he was certain of it even before he went for the knife handle. The cardboard sheath which held the knife was now taped to the top of his forearm. His wrist, in the downward position, could in no way block his draw. He tried it.

Perfect.

He untaped the sheath. There was no need to try it again. Not until the next time—when he had need of the weapon.

The raincoat hanging up to dry, the knife and sheath problem solved, Madden decided his major chores for the day were over.

He thoroughly enjoyed his shave.

Breakfast was bacon and eggs and two more cups of coffee. Around eleven he had the urge for some V-8, but there wasn't any among the kitchen cans. He was out of Scotch, too, and although he knew he wouldn't be drinking today—not until *afterward*—he knew that getting out of the apartment would be good for him, so why not a shopping excursion?

Even the thought of it made his mouth scowl. He'd not shopped for groceries since the marriage, and now . . . and now it might do him some good.

The day still was bright and cheerful as he stepped outside. He noticed that the outer apartment building door caught and locked properly now. Delancy's "word" with the super must have been of much more weight than any of the tenants who had complained. Madden was certain that there had been such complaints; there were simply too many old and crabby women in the place for there not to have been. Good for Delancy. He was an effective cop, in his way.

But not in Madden's way.

He had to orient himself as to which way to go. There was a deli up on Second, but their liquor store was on First. Which way to go first? As he asked the question, it came to him that he'd like nothing more than to take a longer walk—up to the park. Just to see if the kid was still there, or to see what the place looked like, really, in the daylight hours. The idea, of course, was stupid. No, it was more than just stupid. *The criminal always returns to the scene of the crime.* The proverb filled all the old detective books, and whether there was any validity in it or not—he was sure there wasn't—there was no sense at all in his tempting the fates that way.

First, east to the liquor store, then west to the deli. And then back home. To wait until night.

It was a little after eleven when Madden boarded the subway at Lexington and Seventy-seventh. As the train moved southward, he scanned the headlines of the *Post.*

There was no mention of a body being found in Carl Shurz Park. The morning *Times* and the *News* had carried nothing on it as well. He'd picked up both papers at the cornerstand next to the deli, not really expecting to find anything in them, not so much because of the close timing between when the kid with the slit throat might have been found and the papers' deadlines, but because of the fact of the killing itself. Killings weren't all that much news anymore, certainly not knifings in a secluded park.

Thinking that thought earlier in the day, he had wondered whether or not Sara and himself had made the papers. He hadn't looked at a newspaper since last Sunday, and there might have been something—

But he didn't care one way or the other. He'd lunched, showered, slept a couple of hours, had a light dinner, and then had dressed.

Dressed to kill, although not in the popular sense of the phrase.

As the train rumbled down the length of Manhattan, Madden had no eyes for the others who occupied his car. There were two—a black girl, pretty, carrying an artist's leather case, and a small man in an overcoat which looked much too big for him. Having that much data on them both was quite enough for Madden, whose eyes closed. For the tenth or eleventh time that day he was trying again. His location of the book at the apartment had renewed his confidence in his mental recall abilities, and now . . .

In the blank grayness of his mindscreen it came clearly. The wide pink cap, the flash of the knife—and between them the surly, twisted smile and cold and deadly eyes. But the other parts of the face were blurred, as they had been that night. He began focusing in on nostrils which flared backward on chin hair and thick-lobed ears, but he consciously blurred them back, because he knew his imagination was working to try to complete the mind-picture, drawing from any and all sources to help Madden's effort. That nose, for example, was one he recognized as coming directly from one of the photographs in Delancy's book. If he put his mind to it—

Yes. The full face now, a full moon of a negroid face with a patch of light skin discoloration at the top of the left forehead. And the words to the side of the picture: WILLIAMS, WILLY T. And other words describing his career as an armed robber, burglar, small-time drug pusher . . .

But WILLIAMS, WILLY T. wasn't the face Madden wanted to crystallize, and that face he wanted just wouldn't come. Neither that face nor any of the others. He had told Delancy he'd never forget that face, had assured himself it wasn't possible, but it was. He had thought that riding the subway with the sound of the train wheels all around him and the throbbing jostling motion beneath him would help to bring it back, but it wasn't working.

He should have known—did know, in fact—that it wouldn't work. His memory trick, if it was a trick and not the fortunate aberration he thought it was, couldn't be forced. For the most part he could recall anything he'd seen or read, but if he couldn't, there was no use trying. The mental reproduction either came easily or it came not at all. Trying brought nothing into the picture but imagination—sometimes all too clear so as to lead his memory astray for the moment, but only for the moment. There always was a quality—a quality he couldn't quite describe—which labeled the imaginary as false.

No, the pure and simple fact was that he couldn't remember them, any of the four who had killed his Sara. If—maybe if—he saw them again . . .

But what were his chances? The odds were insurmountable that they'd be working the same beat this soon after having narrowly escaped getting caught for a killing. No, that might not be true, either. What in hell did *he* know about the workings of minds such as theirs? Nothing.

He opened his eyes as the train stopped again. Thirty-third. He was getting deeper into battle territory now.

He scowled at the thought. There was no real battle territory, or rather the whole city was battle territory. New Yorkers liked to think that there were some parts of the city which were dangerous and that other parts weren't, but it was purely a matter of degree. The fact of the matter was that the danger areas were wherever it was dark—or wherever you were alone. No, that wasn't even true. The danger areas were where and when the animals decided to strike.

The little man in the outsized overcoat shivered his way out of the car when the train stopped at Astor Place, leaving Madden alone. He rose and checked through the end windows and found that the two cars to the front and rear of his own also were empty. He sat back down and pushed the bottom part of his face into the valley of the trenchcoat lapels. He slouched down, his head leaning over and almost touching his left shoulder, allowing the rhythm of the train to rock it slightly. To any observer he'd look like a man either drunk or extremely worn out after a hard day's work. It didn't make much difference to Madden.

As long as he looked like a good hit.

As the car doors opened at Bleecker, his eyes were alert, flicking back and forth through the narrow slits he allowed himself for vision. Somewhere out on the platform behind him he heard the click of a leather heel on the pavement, followed by another, but he couldn't see who had caused them, and he didn't want to turn fully around. Maybe, though . . . just maybe . . .

But the doors suddenly were closing. *No—not yet; wait!* Madden's brain screamed at the closing panels, but it did no good. They clicked shut and the train again began its southward movement. As it did so, Madden lazily turned his head around to the rear. He saw no one on the platform. Which meant that whoever had been out there moved off.

Or had entered another car.

No sooner had he grasped that thought when the connecting door between his car and that which followed it banged open and shut. Through the slits of his half-closed eyelids Madden made out a figure standing there. A large figure, with a black face, one whose eyes were carefully looking him over, one who stepped forward and stopped directly before him. And spoke:

"You all right, mister?"

Madden nodded. "I'm fine, officer. Just a little tired."

The blue uniformed man with the hand radio unit and the exposed pistol-in-holster didn't look so sure of that, but after a couple of seconds in which Madden felt him weighing the cut and value of his clothing and the polished condition of his shoes, the hefty man in blue grunted something and made his way down to the other end of the car. When the door banged shut, Madden discovered that his right hand was firmly gripping his raincoat just over the left wrist, the fingers of that hand almost frozen in place.

He cursed to himself. He would be unlucky enough to pick a train where John Law was on faithful duty. Where the hell was that bluecoat last Monday night? No, he had to show up now, when—

The train halted. Spring Street. Madden rose to his feet and looked toward the front of the train. If the cop still was in sight . . .

He was, but Madden wouldn't have to get off, because the policeman was doing just that. It was as the doors were closing and Madden's eyes were following the blue uniform's progress across the platform that his eyes caught something else. Another figure, a man who also had been watching the cop, a man who ducked into the shadows behind the stairwell leading up to the open. A black man with a wide mod hat. Not pink, but green. Nonetheless, Madden grinned as the train started up and he watched as the dark patch under the stairwell passed by the window.

He'd found his target for the night.

There weren't that many reasons why a man would hide from a cop who wasn't even coming in his direction. One was that he was a wanted fugitive, but even if that were the case, in a town the size of New York, his chances of being recognized were close to nil—especially by a train cop. Another reason had less to do with what the man had done and more to do with what he was planning. And there weren't all that many things a man could be planning to do hidden in the shadows of a subway platform.

Madden was certain he had his man. There were only a couple of hitches.

One was getting off this train and onto a northbound one fast enough—before his target moved off or found another victim. That was the main hitch. The other—that the man might not try him—he'd worry about that when the time came. First things first.

He got off the southbound at the next stop, Canal Street, and crossed the platform with a hurried walk. As he did so, he noticed there were two black teenagers sitting on a bench some ten yards farther up the platform. They were laughing about something or other, then suddenly the laughing stopped. They had spotted him.

So it's to be here and now? he asked himself. He didn't want it to be. Last night the one he'd gotten was young, tonight he wanted that other one—the one in the shadows. These kids—

What the hell difference did age make! How old were the ones who'd started all this? A killer was a killer regardless of age, and he was at war with all of them.

He turned to face the bench. His eyes caught theirs and he saw them both carefully study his features. He wasn't playing drunk now, his face grim and calm. *All right, folks. If you want it, come and get it.*

He knew deep in his gut that they weren't going to get off that bench. How he knew he couldn't say, but he knew. It was like the night before, when the man in the leather coat had backed off. A certain manner, that's all it took—a manner in which it was obvious that you were just waiting for them to make a wrong move. *I ain't looking for trouble.* He remembered the man in the leather coat saying that, also the others, they said it too. The ones in the subway. And the kid in the park: *Let's not me and you have any trouble . . .*

No, none of them wanted trouble. They wanted things the easy way. They wanted their victims frail or

126

drunk or in some way helpless. And he knew now, as those two black faces scanned his own, that they knew:

He was trouble.

They didn't get up. One of them broke his gaze toward Madden. Madden heard the boy laugh, an uneasy laugh, as he turned and said something to his companion. The other one bobbed his head up and down and laughed back. In two seconds, the way they were swapping jokes again, it was as if Madden wasn't there—almost. Every so often he felt their eyes on him, just for an instant, but on him. Wary eyes, as if they now were expecting *him* to attack. His upper lip curled into a half-smile. The instincts of the jungle animal were not all that bad.

Meanwhile—

Where in hell was that goddamned train!

He had no watch to check, but it seemed an eternity was passing. The one he wanted, the one who was waiting unawares for him, might decide to leave for better pickings. If he did, Madden knew he would curse himself for defying these two now. But all life was a gamble anyway, wasn't it? And if that was the case, it was even more so the case with death.

He heard the rumble on the tracks and looked down into the blackness of the tunnel. No light, nothing. Damn it, the train sound—and the train—was coming from the north! Another southbound train, and—

But wait—there was another rumbling on the tracks. And then he saw the light coming from the southern tunnel, saw it coming closer until the entire engine was in clear view. The two trains stopped almost at the same instant, Madden quickly boarding the one he wanted, then turning to see just what the two teenagers would do now that he was leaving them. With two trains pulled up, there was the possibility they might . . . not his train, probably, but—

Sure enough. Both of them were on their feet now, moving toward the southbound train. He smiled to himself. He was learning how the opposition thought. Not a very complex thinking process, to be sure, not if he could begin to master it in the short time he'd been at it. And then suddenly he decided he had congratulated himself too soon. The two he watched had stopped. They weren't getting on the train after all.

It was when the doors closed on both trains and they started moving that he saw the reason.

There was a cop on that other train.

Madden strained his eyes as the two passing cars picked up speed. He couldn't be sure, but it sure looked like it—

The same cop.

The one who had gotten off his earlier train. If that was the case—and Madden's smile resulted from the almost firm thought that it was—

The smile broadened. His man still would be where he left him. Or he would have been moments ago. Because that cop had been right there on that platform with him, waiting for the next southbound train. Madden's quarry would have had to remain in his shadowy hiding place, and now that John Law had put in an appearance and gone, there was no reason for him to stay right there. The animals, above all others, knew how slim in numbers the cops were. The likelihood of another one coming along soon was close to zero.

Madden quickly sat down and assumed his drunk-exhausted posture. As the train began to slow for the Spring Street stop, he could feel his heart begin to pound. The battle was about to be joined again, and his blood was racing through his system, whether in fear or anticipation, he didn't know. It had been the same years ago in battles in Asia halfway around the world, he remembered. And now he also remembered the method he'd used to calm himself. He blanked out his mind so that no thought could penetrate it except the one he wanted to admit. It was almost a perfect cube, the figure upon which he concentrated. It was completely transparent at first, then it became just a bit cloudy as the light around it faded just a bit, and in that grayness the echo of wind blew white flecks downward and swirling around the huge cube.

Snow, wind-driven and whirling, around the exterior of a large block of ice.

It took only seconds, but by the time the train stopped Madden could release the image. His blood now ran cold within him, his breathing was slow and methodical. And as he rose to cross to the open doors, the pale blue of his eyes were like two frozen, Arctic seascapes. But no one could see them, for once more his head was bowed forward, his face half into the front of his raincoat, as he half-walked, half-staggered from the train and out onto the platform. On the inside he was a calm hair trigger, his muscles and nerves ready to spring to action upon the slightest nudge. On the outside, however—

He stood leaning forward, swaying just a little as the doors closed behind him. He appeared to be trying to figure just which way he should go, now that he was off the train which had begun to move north. His right hand moved up to scratch the top of his head which now was cocked at a peculiar angle as if he were staring at the station sign, as if he were wondering whether he had gotten off at the right stop. Shrugging, he put one foot out after another and moved in an unsure shuffle toward the stairway. He looked as if it took every ounce of effort he had to make it to the bottom, and then he stopped, his head again at an odd angle leaning half onto his left shoulder and peering upward at the long stairs. He was a man who was wondering if it were at all possible to make that impossible climb.

His quarry was very much where he had been, Madden knew. He had seen the dark patch of green when he'd gotten off the train, seen it move back into the blackness. And now as he stood where he did, his right hand seeming to support his left, he could hear the other man's quickened breathing. But there was no other movement from the shadows, no other sound, just the breathing. What the hell was he waiting for? Didn't Madden look easy enough, for Christ's sake? If so, he'd make himself look even easier!

He took a step upward, swayed awkwardly, then forward again as his other foot moved up to the step beyond. "Ha!" he said with a thick tongue. "Made it."

It worked beautifully. He heard the movement from below right, then the man's voice:

"Hey, man. Turn around—real slow."

He knew the man couldn't reach him physically from the distance he maintained, so he was in no hurry to turn. He swayed a bit to his left, then swung his left foot upward onto the next step as if to maintain his balance. He still couldn't see the other man clearly when he muttered out his answer:

"How's 'at?"

"Just turn around. I want your wallet, real careful-like. That way ain't nobody gonna get hurt."

*No trouble, don't want no trouble at all.* Madden had to fight to keep his face under control as he turned the full way around. But as he looked down at the black man with the green hat, the smile he had forced to suppress faded away all by itself.

He was looking square into something he hadn't figured on, into something he knew he should have taken into his calculations.

He was looking square into the barrel of a mean looking handgun.

# ELEVEN

It was something he should have figured on, but something he hadn't. He knew that there were guns all over the city, regardless of the Sullivan Law, which, like most of the laws of society, was obeyed only by the decent people. But he figured guns to be a part of a different crime world—that of the bank robber, the liquor store holdup man, or the Mafia—not the common park or subway vulture. And he'd figured wrong. He'd committed the battlefield sin of underestimating his enemy. It was the kind of error that you didn't often get the chance to make twice.

"Wha . . . ?"

Madden screwed up his face as if he were trying to get a clear look at the thing in the black man's hand.

"Hurry it, man. I ain't got all night." But the voice was cool, and the gunman didn't seem at all hurried. There were no worried looks in any direction to satisfy himself that there was any possible problem on its way from another source. "Come on, buddy—the wallet."

"W-wallop?" Madden said. He was stalling now, a dangerous thing to do, but his mental processes were calculating the range of his possible moves. The revolver was held tightly in the other's right hand, which was extended in bent-arm fashion about three-quarters of an arm's distance from the man's shoulder, the muzzle of the barrel a little more than three feet from Madden's face. A quick step forward and he might be able to block out the gun hand with a forearm slash, but that would have to be done with his left arm, and with that would go his own weapon. True, he'd have the element of surprise in his favor, but—

"Hey? Can't you hear me? I said—"

"Wallet!" Madden said with a thick-tongued exclamation. "Don't hurt me ... It's in my coat ... somewhere . . ."

"Nobody gonna get hurt, man if you do just like I say. Now, where—"

"I don't *know* where . . ." Madden's voice sounded both confused and plaintive at the same time, but his half-closed eyes were watching like those of a hawk. He was fairly sure what the other man would do next, but he decided to help him make up his mind. There was a risk that he might overdo his act, but he counted it a very small risk. *We're smarter than they are,* he reminded himself. "Help me . . . help me find . . ."

"Sure, man, I'll do that. I'll do anything you—*hey, man!*"

But no sooner had the black man's right foot left the ground for the first of the steps than Madden had made his move. It began as a purposely clumsy shift to his own right, but when it ended, it was a full force lunge—his right hand full of gleaming steel. There was an instant when the scene was frozen in time, the black man's mouth open in an almost perfect *O*, the whites of his eyes bulging in disbelief as the victim he had selected came at him—a suddenly changed victim, one who no longer was drunk and staggering but whose terribly scarred face shone like an unholy death which

133

matched that glistening knife which was coming . . . coming . . .

The black man's reflexes moved his chest and stomach out of the path of the knife with a split second to spare. He cried out in triumph as he swung his gun hand around toward Madden, but the cry was followed swiftly by another, and this one had no triumph in it, only pain. At one and the same instant Madden's right knee slammed into the man's wide-open crotch, and the first half-length of his knife sliced into its revised target—into and through the wrist of the swinging gun hand. As the gun clattered onto the stairs, Madden whipped the knife back and took one step backward. Then he brought his left shoetip forward and upward in a vertical arc. The black had been doubled over from Madden's knee and was straightening up fast. He straightened faster when the arc of Madden's shoe cracked into his chin. It was straight up and then over onto his back with a loud and bone-shaking slap to the cement.

He rolled over painfully and pushed himself up to his knees. The first thing he saw was the blood pouring from his right arm. The second thing he saw was the business end of his own pistol.

"Hey, man—no. Come on, now, please—"

The first shot hit him in the left shoulder, slamming him back to the cement. The echo screamed in his ears, drowning out the sound of his own screams. He tried to crawl, but his arms wouldn't function, and he fell onto his face. All he could do now was to try and plead with the crazy white man who had his gun, but he knew . . .

As he looked up into the half-smiling face of that man with the long scar which seemed to be on fire, he didn't have to see the barrel of the pistol rise again to know. Yet he tried to raise his right hand, to ward off—

The second shot entered the black man's head just to the top of the mouth.

The third went dead-center into the forehead.

The gunshots sounded magnified a thousand times in the grayness of the underground tunnel, but the black man was past hearing sound of any kind.

Madden's thumb had cocked the hammer of the revolver, but he now let it come back slowly to rest. There was no need for a fourth shot. The first three had done the job adequately.

His right hand was still in the extended position. He turned his wrist back and forth slowly, his eyes on the gun his fingers held. It had been a long time since he'd held a pistol of any kind, and yet the firing of this one had come so natural, as if it had been only yesterday when the army had drilled him and drilled him . . . Maybe it was like swimming; once you learn you never forget . . .

He took one last look at the dead man sprawled out on the concrete, then he moved to and up the stairwell. He didn't hurry. Why should he? The animals never hurried, so much more reason for the animal slayers to play it cool.

The night air out in the open was refreshingly brisk. Madden walked to the nearest corner. There was a trash bin there, full of old newspapers and wrappings from hot dogs and other waste of the city's earlier hours. With a handkerchief he wiped the revolver clean, then left it under a crumpled *New York Post.* The street seemed empty as he moved from the corner and walked north, hoping to catch a taxi.

He'd reached the middle of the next block when he

stopped. The gun. His first thought had been to get rid of the weapon. It was after all a murder weapon. And the police had ways of telling which gun fired which bullet, the markings on the slug or something. So he'd thought it wise to get rid of the thing which might incriminate him. But now . . .

A gun. How much more effective it was compared to the knife which was strapped to his arm. Quick and clean. Noisy, yes, but who was there to listen—to listen and be curious enough to investigate? And remember, *they* carried the damned things . . .

He walked quickly now, reversing his steps. He was at the trash bin, his left hand encircling the butt of the pistol when he heard the footfalls behind him. His hand remained where it was, but his whole body was at the ready.

The man who stopped some ten feet from him was black and dressed in shabby clothing. A mouth only a third full of teeth grinned at Madden.

"You looking for something, white man?"

Madden's voice was controlled and level. "That's right. How about you?"

The man laughed. It was a sincere, good-natured laugh of a man who meant no harm to anybody.

"Hell, yes, white man. I'm looking, all right. Been looking all my life. But I'll tell you something true."

"What's that?"

The man laughed again. "Whatever it is I'm looking for, I ain't thinking to find it in no trash can."

As the black man turned and walked down the street, shaking his head and laughing, Madden quickly pocketed the pistol and headed in the opposite direction.

Less than a half hour later, he was back in his apartment. During the taxi ride north, he'd made up his mind as to his next moves. The first of them he accomplished as soon as he had sipped from Johnnie Walker's product poured neatly into a champagne goblet. He thoroughly cleaned Sara's butcher knife and retired it back into the kitchen utensil drawer, then he took the cardboard sheath and its tape wrappings and sent it down the shaft in the incinerator room out in the hallway. Then, back in the bedroom, he sipped on the Scotch as he examined his new weapon carefully.

It was a short-barreled Smith & Wesson revolver which carried five bullets. The weapon had been fully loaded tonight, and there were two bullets left in the cylinder—plus three empty shells. He'd have to figure out some way of disposing of those, some way other than dropping them down the incinerator. That was, to coin a phrase, too close to home. Depositing them in separate trash cans or down a sewer would probably be safe enough. He'd worry about that in the morning.

He pushed the pistol under his mattress, then he began to undress. As he did, he caught sight of his reflection in the mirror. Both Maddens nodded to each other.

The war had gotten off to a very good start.

Sat. 9:35

Madden's eyes clicked open and focused onto the digital clock. His left hand snaked over the top of the thing to shut off the alarm and then it pulled back. It wasn't the alarm which was sounding. The phone was ringing. It was old man Chilton:

"How are you feeling, Joe?"

The question took Madden back. He had no idea how to answer it. Fortunately his employer broke the silence without waiting for a response.

137

"What I meant was, are you feeling ready to get back to work?"

Work. He hadn't even thought about it, he'd almost forgotten he had a job, an office. "Mr. Chilton, I don't know. I mean—"

"I know what you mean, Joe." That was good because Madden sure didn't. "But, as I told you when we last spoke, I think the sooner you do get back into the swing of things, the better off you'll be. Besides, things are piling up a little around the office in your absence."

It was the old man's way of telling him that he was needed, something Madden or someone in Madden's circumstances would be expected to want to hear. And it was in fact good to hear it. Aside from his new job, his new purpose, there was a part of him which wanted to get back to the office drawing board. The war he'd just begun was a simple, elemental war. His work at Chilton and Harris was a more sophisticated war, one against inefficiency and waste, one which employed more complex strategies.

"I think, Joe, that you ought to consider it. No pressure, you understand—and I mean this sincerely. Take as much time as you feel you need, but—"

"Monday," Madden said.

"What's that, Joe?"

"I said Monday. If that's all right, I think I'd like to come in Monday. You're right. I think I do need to get back to some kind of—" He couldn't think of the word, not one which fit.

"Normalcy," Chilton completed the sentence, but that wasn't exactly right, either. Things never would be normal again, not in the old sense. But Madden accepted the word.

"Right. Normalcy."

There were a couple of more short exchanges which were intended to end the conversation gracefully, but they didn't exactly come off. Finally, though, Madden's telephone was back on the hook.

He was out in the kitchen starting the coffee when the telephone rang again.

"Joe? Leo Delancy. How—"

"I'm fine, Leo. Fine as I can be, that is."

"You sound good, Joe. I—er—tried to call you last night." A pause. "You go out or something?

His mind examined the alternatives. He could say he was at home and had let the phone ring because he hadn't wanted to talk to anybody. He could say that, but that conjured up a picture of a brooding, self-pitying man, and as Delancy had said, he sounded good this morning. Too good to use that story.

"I went out. I'd had enough of staying cooped up. I had to get out."

Another pause. "But sober this time, I hope."

"Sober as a judge—or a cop."

"Joe . . ." This time the pause was even more obvious. Delancy was after something, and Madden thought he knew what it was. He decided to let the man wait a while.

"Leo, how did it go? You know, with the ring and the watch. You turn up anything?"

"Not yet, but I'm hopeful. They're not the kinds of things these people would keep. Too expensive to wear, I mean. No, they'll be trying to pass them for cash sooner or later. I'm hopeful."

"Then I'll be hopeful, too."

There was another silence, then Delancy:

"Joe, I have to admit I was worried about you. You

know, the other night, the way you were talking and all . . ."

There it was, the thing Delancy was after, the thing Madden had known was coming. He'd played it stupid then, he decided to play it dumb now.

"The way I was talking?" he said.

"Yeah. Like . . . well, like you were going to do something—on your own."

"On my own?" He had to be careful now, careful not to overplay the confusion bit.

"You know, like a . . . like an avenger or something. You were talking about doing something to sort of . . . well, square things—"

"Oh," Madden said, as if dimly recalling what they'd talked about. "I guess I did say some stupid things. I'm sorry if—"

"Sorry? You've got nothing to be sorry about."

This time it was Madden's turn to pause. Was he reading Delancy wrong? Was the big cop—did he *approve,* deep down, of what Madden had—

No. Delancy's next words brought that home:

"Hell, Joe—everybody talks like that at one time or another. In your case you had every reason to sound off. I just wanted to make sure that—"

"That better judgment prevailed?"

"Yeah, something like that."

"I start work again Monday," Madden said.

"Good. That's real good. The sooner you get back to doing what you do for a living, the better off you'll feel. Feeling useful can do a lot to heal the wounds, Joe, I can tell you that from personal experience. Something else, too. Your wife's stuff."

"How's that?"

"Her things. Her clothes and jewelry, that sort of

stuff. The sooner you get rid of it—I mean, I know this sounds kind of hard-nosed, Joe, but I know what I'm talking about. The sooner you get rid of her everyday things, the better it will be for you. I don't mean everything—not pictures of her, not that sort of thing—but her clothes and stuff. You know."

Madden looked around the place. Delancy was right. He would never forget Sara, but she would be the last person in the world to want icons all over the place for him to sorrow over.

"I'll call her sister. Maybe she—"

"Good idea, Joe." Another short silence, then: "Joe, I'm real glad you're taking this the way you are."

Madden didn't quite know the right tone to use, but he settled on something between a wryness and a sadsardonic. "You mean, not taking to the streets like some kind of Boston Strangler."

"That's right."

"I learned my lesson, Leo. Like you said, I was lucky my face slicing stopped where it did. Besides, it's not only knives they've got out there—it's guns too, right?"

The sudden turn of his conversation was the result of his realizing that he needed some information and that the man on the other end of the line was in one of the better positions to get it from.

"That's true. We have our share of shootings."

"The thing is," Madden said, "I can't figure how they get them. A gun—okay, I can figure that. But guns need bullets. Somehow I just can't picture one of these small-bit hoodlums ordering up boxes of shells over the counter at Abercrombie and Fitch."

Delancy laughed at the image. Madden had hoped he would. "No, Joe, they get what they get easily, nonetheless. Money will buy anything you want in this city. All you have to do is be in the right dark bar or bright-lit poolhall with the right amount of money, and the right supplier will be along without much of a delay."

"Seems to me," Madden said matter-of-factly, "you ought to clean out a few dark bars and bright-lit pool-halls."

"We do our best, Joe, we do our level best."

There was only one more thing of any essence which Delancy brought up. Madden's stitches. They ought to come out Monday or Tuesday at the latest. "How's the scar looking?" he asked.

"Not bad," Madden said with a dry voice. "Looks like one side of my face has aged a little more than the other, that's all."

When Delancy was off the line, Madden got out Sara's little white address book. He found her sister's work number without difficulty. Her voice sounded as apologetic and small as ever, but she saw the wisdom of his desire to get rid of Sara's things.

"Tomorrow would be fine, Joe," she said. "I'll take everything you want to get rid of, and anything that doesn't fit or that I can't use I'll give to Goodwill or some other charity."

"No, Jean." His voice was dead cold. "You'll take what you want, but what you can't use, don't take. What you don't take goes right down the incinerator."

"But Joe—"

"That's final. You get what you want. The bastards who killed Sara—them and their kind—get nothing. Nothing from Sara," he amended.

He lunched downtown, at the Bottom of the Sixes, treating himself to two martinis before deciding to order his club sandwich. They tasted good. Well they should, he thought to himself. It was, in a way, a celebration, although maybe just a little premature. He'd managed to throw Delancy off the scent—if the cop had been on the right one at all—and he'd gained an important piece of information from the man. Another piece of information was in the book he now opened flat on the table. He'd bought it at Brentano's. *Gun Digest*, containing pictures and the relevant statistics of the offerings of the major gun manufacturers of America and abroad.

Under the Smith & Wesson collection he found it:

## SMITH & WESSON 38 CHIEFS SPECIAL & AIRWEIGHT

| | |
|---|---|
| Caliber: | 38 Special, 5 shot. |
| Barrel: | 2 inches, 3 inches. |
| Length: | 6½ inches (2″ bbl. and round butt). |
| Weight: | 19 oz. (2″ bbl.; 14 oz. AIRWEIGHT). |
| Stocks: | Checkered walnut, Magna. |
| | Round or square butt. |
| Sights: | Fixed, $\frac{1}{10}$″ serrated ramp front, |
| | square notch rear. |

The picture above the description was exactly the same as the revolver now resting comfortably under his mattress. Round butt, a two-inch barrel. Whether his weapon was the nineteen or fourteen ounce model was unknown. And unimportant.

After lunch, he walked down Fifth Avenue to Korvettes. There he went straight to the housewares department where he bought a pair of plastic gloves. They were the see-through kind, skin tight. No impediment to finger movement, but a real protection against fingerprints—in the event that Chiefs Special some night didn't make it back under that mattress safely.

# TWELVE

Saturday night in New York City. Somewhere behind closed apartment doors and windows the people of the city are making love, quarreling, quietly reading Chaucer or *Screw* magazine, eating gourmet meals, or getting plastered on cheap red wine. The bright lights of downtown lure others into the dim lights of places where there is dancing, hand-holding, and whispers of promises which only will be partially fulfilled during the hours ahead. In other dimly lit places to the north and south and east and west there is the smell of marijuana in the air, the small sound of a dirty needle piercing arm skin, the tastelessness of a yellow or red or green capsule being swallowed. And in the great concrete canyons which separate all of these places there is violence or the threat of violence or violence about to happen.

Innocent people, good people, will die tonight. But so will some of those who are not innocent, especially on the lower East Side.

The bartender looked up casually as Madden sat down, then took another look in the sick-red and yellow lighting of the neon which burned out the name of a popular beer over the broken clock on the wall behind him. Madden didn't notice the name of the beer. He was, however, interested in the second look the bartender gave him. The expression on the man's face was the right one.

It showed unease, readiness. As if he thought Madden might be trouble. And that was exactly the way Madden wanted to appear. Tonight, in this lower Tenth Avenue bar, he wanted precisely to look like nobody to mess around with. The taut expression on his face and the steel-like look in his eyes helped, but he knew that the scar was the clincher. And so it had been in the two previous bars he'd visited tonight.

"Help you, mister?" the bartender asked. Madden didn't fail to notice that the man's right hand was out of sight under the bar.

"Maybe," he said. "Scotch and a favor."

The bartender, a heavy man whose beefy face looked like it might have served as a punching bag in John L. Sullivan's training camp, took his eyes off Madden only long enough to pour the Scotch. Madden took the opportunity to look around the place. The nine-thirty crowd amounted to four other customers. One small man at the other end of the bar, a couple in their fifties in a booth, and in another, at the far end of the room, concentrating in the candle light on something on the table in front of him, a thin rat-faced man.

"Scotch," said the bartender. He set the drink before Madden and then moved away. But his eyes were still on the new customer.

"There was something else," Madden said.

"What would that be?"

Madden's lips curled. "For twenty bucks, I'd like it kept out of the public domain."

The bartender moved in closer. "Twenty bucks? What's worth twenty bucks?"

"Not Scotch, not when it's served in a dirty glass," Madden said.

The barkeep laughed nervously, not sure how to take Madden. "That's pretty good. I liked your other one, too. Out of the public domain. Real uptown talk."

Madden placed the crisp new twenty on the bar. He had paid out a similar bill at the last place. Information was an expensive commodity in the jungle. "I was told Joey Marbles comes in here sometimes."

"Who?"

"I have to repeat myself, and you get half of twenty."

"What you want with Joey?"

"Joey will tell you later, if he wants you to know. You earn your twenty by getting him here quick like a bunny."

"You a friend of Joey's?"

"I never laid eyes on him. I want to. Do you get my twenty or do you keep asking stupid questions?"

The barkeep's face flushed hot then cold then hot again. Nasty words were welling up in his throat, and Madden considered it a tribute to his acting ability—and his scarred face—that the nastiness stayed welled up.

"Okay," Madden said. "But when I do find Joey, I'll tell him how cooperative you were." He reached for the bill.

"Wait. Okay—let me check with somebody first, okay?"

He didn't wait for an answer, but moved down to the opposite end of the bar and out the gate there—straight into the booth area and to the rat-faced man. They were still whispering, both of them studiously avoiding looking back at the bar, when Madden placed his drink on the table. The bartender jumped as if he'd been shot.

146

The rat-face betrayed no emotion at all, simply eyes watching eyes. Madden's eyes dropped to the table. He smiled. The thing the Rodent had been studying so intensely was a backgammon board, open and pieces arranged in mid-play.

"It's in vogue," Rat Face said. His voice sounded like a rough grade of sandpaper slowly pushed along a blackboard.

Madden shoved past the bartender and sat down. He looked up at the beefy face. "Mr. Marbles and I would prefer to be alone."

The bartender looked to Rat Face for instructions. Rat Face nodded only once. "It's okay, Mike. I'll talk to the gentleman." When Mike was once more behind the bar, the Rodent nodded again and moved some of the backgammon pieces. He shook his head, frowning, then pulled his beady eyes to Madden's.

"Who says I'm this Marbles guy?"

Madden's stare was relaxed but unblinking. "Let's say you're not Joey Marbles. I don't care who the hell you are. I just want something that you might be able to supply. Fifty rounds of thirty-eight ammo to grace the insides of a Chiefs Special."

"That's a cop's gun," Rat Face observed. His eyes stayed where they were, his tone disinterested.

"Maybe it belonged to a cop once. Right now it's mine and empty. Fifty rounds, Joey. Tonight."

The eyes dropped. More pieces of the game shifted. Another frown. "I didn't say I was Joey. And I don't know about getting ammo. What makes you think I might?"

Madden's voice now was tight. "Look, pal. I got the word passed to me that you were a man to see. I got a need, see? A real need. I got this little job assigned to me, but I need some things to complete it. If you don't supply me, and I find out you *could* have . . ." Madden grinned. It was not a nice grin. "Then, Joey boy, I just might get the urge to do a freebie, just to even the score. You follow what I'm saying?"

Rat Face's eyes dropped again, but Madden didn't miss the slight tremor in the man's hand as it moved another piece.

"You could be a cop."

"You could be dead tomorrow, Joey."

"You got nothing against me." But his eyes raised to see how Madden took the statement.

Madden smiled. "That's right, Joey, I got nothing against you—if you get me what I need. Otherwise, what I got is a bad taste in my mouth, and I don't like bad tastes."

Almost a complete minute passed before the Rat nodded. "If I had a source, *if*, they wouldn't come cheap."

Two fifty dollar bills suddenly appeared on the backgammon board. Madden slid out of the booth. "Have my package for me here—in twenty minutes."

"Twenty—"

"You heard, Joey."

"Look—" Rat Face stood. He was taller than Madden had thought, but as lean as a skeleton. "Look, I mean, twenty minutes. I'm not sure that I can—"

Madden smiled his nasty smile. "Okay, Joey. You got a half hour. No more, not a second more. Thirty minutes from now, if you're not back here with the merchandise, I figure you've skipped with my bills. From that time on you can count the number of hours you got left to you in this life."

The slight tremor Madden had noticed before had

148

graduated into a full-fledged shudder. He couldn't help but notice, the way the two fifties were fluttering in front of his face.

"Look—you hold onto these. I'll collect when I—"

"No sale, Joey. You pocket them—now. I don't want any money passing hands when you bring me my package, wrapped in a plain paper bag. After all," he grinned coldly, "you might be trying to do me in."

"Huh?"

"How do I know, Joey? You might be a cop."

Twenty-five minutes later Madden was sipping his second Scotch when Rat Face came back into the bar. He didn't look at Madden as he took a stool two down from Madden's own. Madden drained the Scotch, then stood. Then his fingers closed around the brown paper bag which the nervous skeleton had placed on the stool between them.

"See you around, Joey," he said. As Madden left the bar, he wondered whether he would.

He didn't wonder long. It wasn't all that important. It was Saturday night and still early according to the city's customs. He was on the streets.

And on those streets, there were others.

# THIRTEEN

His pale white face was gaunt and pockmarked, his black hair combed back into a ponytail. As he sat in the apartment lobby, his eyes were watchful, unaware that other eyes were watching his own. Twice now he had let potential victims pass, the first man looking as if he weighed about two-sixty and could break into small bits both the switchblade knife he had in his pocket as well as himself. Sure enough, the guy proved he was a heavy athlete by not giving the elevator a second glance but taking the stairs to their right two at a time. He didn't stop at the second floor, either. Then came the woman, young and carrying two suitcases—she might have been an easy target, if it hadn't been for the mean looking man who rushed through the door after she opened it. The two of them weren't together, but he had no liking to try, not while the man was there. And he—the man—went into the elevator with the woman, looking at the bench where he sat as if amused, as if daring him to try something.

Hell. He didn't need to take any dares. All he had to do was wait. The silly bastards don't challenge you when you come in behind them—opening their precious front door locks with their precious keys—and later, if you select the right target, you don't get challenged then, either. You get paid. Sometimes more, sometimes less, but whatever you got it was pretty good pay for doing nothing but sitting on your butt and waiting.

Tonight, though . . .

He felt a little uneasy. He didn't know why, but he did. But, hell, he'd worked this area for weeks and there hadn't been any trouble, and there was no reason to expect there would be any tonight.

Uneasy. Why? Because of the waiting? No, he'd had to wait longer than this before. You had to wait, to sit quietly, minding your own business—until the chicken—the exactly right chicken—came your way.

He called them that. The chickens. And he, of course, was the Chicken Hawk. Swooping down on the farmyard and plucking them—one by one, night after night. But you had to be careful that the Rooster, his term for the fuzz or for anybody else who might take a hand, wasn't out in the yard but instead tucked away, far away out of sight.

The front door opened and the Chicken Hawk smiled to himself. The man entering was old and tottering. He looked like he was a hundred and eighty-seven if he was a day. But his clothes were good, and the Hawk could make out the bulge of the old man's wallet in his left breast pocket.

A Chicken of veritable gold! All these old farts carried their money on them—in wads. They were afraid somebody might break into their pads and make off with what Social Security allowed them to hide away each month. Old-agers worrying about their security—when they got still older. Christ, they should realize that it wasn't old Chickens who needed money—it was the young Hawks.

He waited until the old man pushed the elevator button. Then the Hawk stood. At the snap of the knife, the Chicken turned around so fast he almost tore his own neck off. His eyes showed fear. It was good. The Hawk always felt good when he saw their fear. It stopped them from doing anything crazy, that was part of it, but to be honest with himself, he knew he enjoyed seeing them cringe for its own sake. It was raw power—his power.

"W-what do you want?" the old geezer asked. But he knew already what the Hawk wanted. His right hand instinctively went to the left breast of his coat. The old Chicken thought he could hide his bread with that shaking, spindly old arm.

"Your money—or your life!" the Hawk sneered. He'd used the line since he first saw it in an old flick about an English or Irish highwayman. He liked it, especially when they already were scared. It was direct, and it was efficient communication. "Now," he added.

The old man's eyes looked at the sharp tip of the knife, his hands trembling but not moving as ordered.

"Hey, Chicken—your hearing aid out of order or something? I don't like wasting my time."

*"That's good because you don't have much left to waste!"*

It was the Hawk's head which now snapped up. There on the third or fourth of the stairs was the man who had come in earlier—the one who'd followed behind the woman with the suitcases. He hadn't noticed before just how big that scar was on the bastard's face. Something else the Hawk hadn't seen before:

The gun in the man's hand—a hand wrapped in plastic or something.

"He-he's trying to rob me!" the old man bleated.

"I know that, sir," the man with the gun said.

The Hawk knew he'd had it. He'd been caught with the goods. He considered grabbing the old man and using him as a shield, but it wouldn't work. The pistol looked cocked and ready to fire. From the look on that scarred face, if the Hawk tried anything quick, it would be all over.

The knife went *clack* on the lobby floor. He put his hands in the air and stepped slowly toward the gun. "Okay, man. It looks like you got—"

The roar of the pistol interrupted him. He screamed as his hands went up to his face where there was now a wet and gaping hole, his back slamming against the wall as the bench caught him at the inner knees. He sat down hard, his hands coming away from his face just long enough to see the gunman turn to the old Chicken.

"I hope you're all right, sir."

"I am—*now*," the old man answered.

The Hawk screamed again as he saw the hole in the pistol barrel swing and stop inches from his eyes. Then his world exploded into a thousand colors, all of which turned into the deadest of black.

The woman screamed, trying to defend herself. She was over forty and was a hefty woman, Latin looking. Her attacker also looked Latin, but he was much younger, in his late teens or early twenties. He wasn't armed, or if he was, he wasn't using a weapon of any kind—only his hands, which were closing tightly around the woman's throat. She was trying her best to beat him off with her pocket book, but she did not have a quarter of the strength that the boy was using against her. Then suddenly his hands released her. He seemed as if to fly, his

153

feet lifting from the pavement and his body diving wildly to her right.

There was a loud crash then—no, two crashes. The first was like the sound of thunder. The second was the attacker's loud collision with a line of trash cans.

Her tearful eyes swept to her left. She gasped. There was a man standing there, a pistol in his hand. She could not see his face in the shadows, and somehow she knew she didn't want to, knew that it was a face she should not see. She looked at the still body of the one who had leaped at her from the darkness, and then she looked at the other man, the man who now had turned his back and was walking away from her.

*"Valgate Dios!"* she called after him. "May God bless you!"

Madden, his gun shoved deep into his raincoat, thought the blessing very appropriate.

It was, after all, Sunday morning.

# FOURTEEN

Sunday morning.

Jean said she would come by sometime after ten-thirty so Madden went out for the papers earlier. The *News* and *Times* were silent as to his exploits, but in a Saturday *Post* which he'd fished out of a trash can at the corner, he found an item that interested him:

### MOB-STYLE HIT DROPS PAROLEE

Three bullets and a knife slash ended the life of LeRoy Lenox, 30, last night about midnight on the cold concrete Spring Street platform of the Lexington subway line.

Lenox, who in his youth was a leader of Harlem's Savage Knights teenage gang, was released from prison in August after serving three years of a ten-year term for armed robbery. The original indictment had been for first degree murder, but Lenox pleaded guilty to the lesser charge. It was the second trip to prison for Lenox, who in 1965 was released after serving four years on a robbery conviction.

An official source theorizes that Lenox was killed by at least two, possibly three, attackers. None of the dead man's personal effects appeared to have been taken.

Madden grinned over his glass of V-8. So now he was a mob! Good enough. He didn't crave anything in the way of publicity. But it was nice to know that he'd taken out a probable murderer as well as whatever else the late Mr. LeRoy Lenox had been. As for the dead man's effects, one of them had come in very handy—and would continue to do so, as long as he could feed it properly. The feeding was expensive, there was no doubt about that. Not counting the forty bucks to get to the Rodent, the fifty rounds he'd bought had cost him two dollars apiece. On that basis, he ought to be more conservative in their use. The punks he'd taken out last night had cost him a total of six bucks.

Madden laughed. What the hell was money for? Besides he'd gotten the gun for nothing.

When Jean showed, Dan came along with her. He looked sheepish as he accepted Madden's offer of coffee while Jean went through Sara's things.

"Joe—I really am sorry, I really am, about the other day."

Madden nodded. Hell, the poor slob did really mean it, and he couldn't really help being what he was. Dan might be obnoxious or whatever else, but he didn't go around mugging other people. "It's okay, Dan. I should be the one apologizing. I sort of flew off the handle."

"I should've kept my big mouth shut, I really should've."

Madden saw no reason to comment. He noticed, however, that Dan was looking at him as if he wanted to say something further—or to ask something. He wasn't sure what it was all about until Jean came back into the living room. Her face had looked uncomfortable since she'd entered his apartment, and it still looked that way, but now her eyes told him the question on both his in-law's minds. She was looking directly at his scar. It was something new since they'd last seen him.

"Little accident," he said, trying to smile cheerfully and pass it off. "Nothing serious."

"It sure looks serious, Joe," Dan said. "I didn't want to ask or nothing, but if you need to see a good doctor—"

"I'll be seeing one tomorrow or Tuesday—to get the stitches out." He suddenly realized that he didn't have a doctor in town. Sara had been to one, but he doubted that a gynecologist would relish this kind of work. He'd make it a point to get a recommendation from Chilton or somebody else at the office.

"Looks like it was a real mean cut," Dan said. "How—"

A sharp look from Jean stopped him. Madden decided he'd better say something. He didn't intend to see much of these two people in the future; no sense making this meeting any worse than it was.

"Stupid accident," he said, waving a hand toward the kitchen. "Nobody should play around with opening a can when they're half smashed—or, as in my case, more than half smashed."

Dan nodded. "Yeah. Those metal cuts can be real rough. I remember once, this guy I knew a few years back—"

But Jean didn't want to listen. "Joe, I've got everything I can use. About the other things—I mean, well,

157

Sara's shoes. They don't fit me, but it seems a shame, they're so nice and all. I was thinking—"

"You've got a friend who could use them?"

"Well, no, not that. What I meant was, well, there are plenty of people in need who—"

"No, Jean."

"But Joe—"

"I said no. They—and everything else you don't take for yourself—go down into the incinerator. Today."

"Joe, listen. You can't blame everybody for—"

He stood, the look on his face freezing her mouth in its open position. "It's not open for debate, Jean."

She looked away from him. "I . . . I just thought that Sara . . . well, that she would want . . ."

Madden's features softened a bit. "Maybe she would have wanted things your way. I think you might be right about that. But no, Jean. No."

It took them two trips down to the car to complete the transfer of Sara's things to her sister. When everything was loaded, Dan extended his hand to Madden.

"I don't guess we'll be seeing much of each other, Joe." His expression was a little sad, sincerely so.

Madden took the hand. Dan's grasp was firm, but not the he-man bone-crushing type of thing which had been his trademark. "Take care, Dan," Madden said. That was all. He could think of nothing else.

It was after the car drove off that Madden realized he'd not said goodbye to Jean. Somehow he felt sorry about it, more specifically he felt sorry about his feeling that not having said goodbye didn't matter, that she didn't matter. It was wrong, somehow. People, no matter who, ought to matter.

He felt very alone at that moment. Alone and lonely and empty.

He continued to feel that way as he fed the rest of Sara's things down the incinerator. Along with them went the newspapers, including the news-style obituary of LeRoy Lenox.

The next two hours he spent cleaning the apartment. Of Sara's things, there was hardly anything left. Pictures, mostly. Pictures of the two of them laughing, happy. Pictures of her alone, portraits of love and beauty. Pictures of him, proud and content and—

He put them in a drawer which Jean had emptied, all except one of the photographs. It was taken on Park Avenue. Madden had posed her with the Pan Am Building in the background. The girl and the city, that was his title for it. It was before they were married, and it had been his favorite picture of her. He had forgotten the photo and the taking of it, and as he now sat on the bed, the picture in his hand, he wondered whether he would forget the woman herself. He didn't ever want to forget her, he didn't want to forget even one of the happy moments they shared, painful as the remembering might be.

And then the empty feeling hit him full force.

He placed the photograph of Sara on the chest of drawers. Then he cleaned the revolver and made a fresh pot of coffee.

The coffee tasted good, very good. And somehow he felt good. Maybe because it was Sunday.

The seventh day. Of the week, and since the night on the train when Sara was taken from him. He had lived without her almost a full seven days this Sunday. The Lord's day, his day of rest. And so it had been with Madden and his wife—a day of rest, of a late Bloody

159

Mary brunch, of reading the Sunday *Times*, either in bed or when weather permitted on the grass of Central Park.

It was a nice day, a bright day in which the weather was balmy for this time of year. The thought of Central Park remained with Madden as he sipped his coffee. Yes, it would be good to walk among the trees and grass. He above all didn't want to spend this day, this Sunday, alone in the apartment.

It was just after one when he left the apartment. He didn't hurry. He knew he had the entire day to get through, and he did not want to rush anything. For he would have the night ahead of him as well, and tonight wasn't going to be another night of the hunt. The seventh day would be his day of rest as well.

He crossed Second Avenue, his pace quickening, his breathing deep. The sunshine, the Sunday-clean air, the unusual warmth of the day made him feel strangely good inside. He felt, perhaps for the first time in what seemed an eternity, human. Alive and human and well. It was as if some magic of the daylight itself had touched him, as if he had been mysteriously awakened from a nightmare world of horrors.

A world of dark streets, that other world ... of startled faces ... of quick death. And he, the vigilante stalker, dealing out punishment to the leeches of the night.

*Vengeance is mine, saith the Lord.*

Those were Sunday words, appropriate to the day, and maybe the words were more valid than Madden had thought. His Sara was gone; there was no way of bringing her back, none. The empty place he felt within him—

That would stay, always. No matter how many of them he killed.

How many.

As he crossed Lexington he thought about it. He couldn't recall just how many of them there had been. He had to review them in his mind. The blond kid, the first. Then came LeRoy Lenox. Then, last night, two more. Four. He shook his head. Not at the number itself but at the fact that he'd had to count them one by one. He'd killed four people and he had to stop and think to remember just how many of them there were.

Madden of the memory. Was he beginning to lose his grip?

*Vengeance is mine . . .*

As he waited for a sudden line of cars to pass before crossing Park Avenue, he inhaled deeply. Was it over? Had the need to kill passed? Maybe it had. Maybe when he returned home this afternoon he could resolve himself to getting rid of the pistol and the dearly purchased bullets. Maybe. In the meantime, there was this warm Sunday afternoon . . . and the park.

Madden walked up to the Seventy-ninth Street entrance, but even before he turned left onto the roadway he saw that his fellow citizens in great numbers felt the way he did about this strange day which had been given them in the midst of this normally unkind month of the year. They were everywhere, walking hand in hand, biking, jogging, chasing children or dogs or both— young and old, richly dressed and poorly. Couples even were sitting on the grass—reading the *Times.* They were lucky, Madden reflected. Lucky to have each other to read interesting items to, to laugh with, to love. As for himself . . .

It was true, even with his sorrow: he felt good to be alive. And for those he'd killed . . .

It was not remorse he felt, nor was it any sense of guilt. He had struck out because he'd had to, his sanity had demanded it. Those he had struck down deserved to die. No, that wasn't exactly true. What was true was that they didn't deserve to live. There was a difference, at least in Madden's mind, even though he found it difficult to sort out just what that difference was. He wasn't even sure that he had felt that way about them when he'd killed them. But today, in the Sunday sunlight, he felt that way. Maybe it was because they, as creatures of the night, could—should—have no part in this world of civilization. His removal of them was a cleansing of the city, part of a more deadly, anti-litter campaign.

He shrugged it off. He didn't want to think about it.

The path he walked passed by the supposedly three thousand-year-old obelisk called Cleopatra's Needle. It looked its full three thousand years old, probably as the result of pollution getting to its surface, but it didn't look much like anybody's needle. But then, things are rarely what they seem. Did he, Joe Madden—as he walked leisurely through the patches of sunlight beneath the trees—did he look like the slayer of four? That elderly woman who was returning his smile now, could she ever have a hint of who he was and what he had done?

Again he shrugged off the thought.

The New Lake now was on his left and to his far left the curious Belvedere Castle, one of Sara's favorites. She'd told him that just looking at it made her feel like some kind of storybook princess. Looking at it from below, that is. Once she had gained the top of it, the illusion had vanished for her, and it was no more than a weather-beaten weather station. To Madden himself the building had said nothing at all, but he'd gone along with her myth-making. "You are the fair princess and I the knight. Bewitched by your beauty, I repeat your name and go forth to slay dragons—"

To slay them dead.

No. He'd done his slaying. The city had yielded four of its dragons to his death-hand. He had done his knight's job, now he had another job to go to. The first thing in the morning, tomorrow, he would again be Engineer Joe Madden. Tomorrow night—maybe tonight—he'd take the gun and the bullets and drop them—

In the river.

Those were the last three words he needed to complete the thought which was about to become his resolve.

He never completed it.

The walkway was not overly crowded ahead. He could see the Delacourt Shakespeare Theater directly in front of him some twenty yards, but that was out of just the corners of his eyes. His main point of focus was the scene which had switched his mind off the channel it had been on.

A woman—late thirties—suddenly screaming. A man with the woman—a fat round man weighing in at what must have been two-eighty—grasping his chest right over his heart, his face a bad shade of light blue. And a third figure—a young black holding a camera, an expensive looking thing with a long telephoto lens—a young black running like hell.

*"Stop him!"* the woman screamed.

Madden's feet moved. The black, in a black leather jacket, ran directly north, at a right angle from the path

163

Madden had been on. But he no longer was on that path, his shoes pounding the turf as he took up the chase. *"Stop him!"* he yelled, but no one moved to obey him. There were people there, none of them in very clear focus, but they were there. Several of them stopped still as stone statues, others just looked at him as if he were crazy and kept walking. The point was— no one moved to intercept the black kid!

And the kid could run—his long thin legs moving out one after the other, pushing him between the trees and wide around clusters of people as if he were going hell-bent for the end zone. As they moved north across the great lawn the distance between the boy and Madden widened. Ten yards, fifteen, then twenty, then . . .

Madden lost sight of him. He pushed himself all the harder, yelling for somebody, anybody: *"Stop the kid with the camera!"*

And then Madden stopped. There was no sense to anymore running. He'd lost the bastard and that was that. He turned back toward the Shakespeare theater, his heart pounding at its still quick pace, his face flushed with exertion, his eyes fiery with rage.

There was a crowd around the fat man on the path-way. His wife was sobbing, mumbling the words "his poor heart" and others which only she and the heavens could understand. There was a uniformed policeman bending over the fallen man, asking the people to move back.

"Move back, goddamn it!" Madden said through his teeth. He reached out and grabbed two shoulders and pulled. One of the shoulders went past him all the way to the ground. The other shoulder owner moved his feet fast enough to avoid the fall, but he—a heavy kid in his own right—didn't bother moving back into his prior position. He couldn't. Madden was there now and pushing other people aside.

"Didn't you hear the man? He said *move the hell back!*"

His eyes then caught those of the cop. The face under the cap was young, inexperienced. It looked uncomfortable. When Madden looked at the face of the fat man, he thought he knew why.

It probably was the first time the young officer had seen a dead man.

Nine thirty-five. That was the time when Madden again slipped into the Seventy-ninth Street entrance to the park and moved quickly into the thickest of the shadows available. Anywhere else in the city, the night was young for what he had in mind, but not here. Here in Central Park there was still the ten o'clock curfew in effect, a wise policy of the city fathers to keep the law-abiding out of the danger which was Central Park at night. The policy, of course, was only half-effective since the lawless, after ten, had only themselves to prey upon—themselves and the old worn out men of many successive cheap drunks, old cast-offs of society who offered the animals no gain other than convenient means of psychological kicks. Beating up the bums was a fun thing, but it wouldn't be tonight, not if Madden was nearby.

Still, it was only nine thirty-five. Madden did not know the time exactly, and he made a mental note that he would buy a watch during the lunch hour tomorrow. It bothered him not to know the time, although he knew he still would have a chance to draw the bastards' attack to himself. They would be in there now, he knew—waiting. Hoping that there would be some sucker who, having an appointment to meet someone across town and also having a negative view regarding the high cost of taxis, would decide on the very legal but very dangerous expedient of quickstepping through the park.

They would be here—here at Seventy-ninth where the pathway crossed almost in a direct slice to West Eighty-first, here where the hurried pedestrian would move across the dark expanse by the shortest route. Here, and to the south they would be waiting along the path that connected East Sixty-ninth with its western counterpart. They would be here waiting, not for the drunks and already destroyed men in rags. No, those would be available for recreation after ten. Now it was open season on any of the straights foolish enough to wander into the kingdom of the animals.

Madden stood still, listening, looking. Not for *them*, but for the police who patrolled the park with regularity. They also knew the name of the game, but the park was large and the stalkers after prey were many. In this jungle—because of the police—there was only one strategy followed by the animals. Kill and kill quick—before the prey had a chance to scream or put up a fuss which would bring down the law.

The law.

Where had it been this afternoon? There, yes, but too late. Too late to apprehend the criminal, too late to prevent the fat man's dying from heart failure. That black kid this afternoon had violated something, something which Madden's mind had raised to the almost sacred. He had brought it back in full force. The enforcers of the law were helpless in stopping the violators. The ethics of civilization were not recognized by, and thus did not apply to, the savages of the jungle. Therefore, there was no escaping it.

166

Only another savage could restore some sense of balance. Only another savage who was as ruthless as they. They were judges, juries and executioners, and so he too would be. But he had an advantage. He knew them. They, on their part, could not hope to know him, could not be dimly aware or comprehend that one of the helpless prey had grown talons and fangs and was hunting them down on their own turf.

Justice is mine, saith the Lord.

Saith Madden: Lord, you've got some help. It would be best to get some authorization for the job, but I don't know where to file.

He saw nothing, heard nothing, and it was time to start. He planned to move fast—a man in a hurry, a man just a little frightened by the passage through the park at night. They were there and they'd strike, he was certain of it. He had taken two steps out of his hiding place when he heard something that pulled him back.

Footsteps.

Loud footsteps. Moving swiftly like he had planned to move, but coming down on the pavement before the path almost too quickly. And then he saw why. Why they were swift and shy and clicked as loudly as they did.

It was a woman.

She was nicely dressed, her skirt short enough to show a good length of shapely leg. She wore fur and carried an oversized handbag as she moved from the pavement onto the pathway. Still her heels clicked loudly on the asphalt, sending a message ahead that the night hunters couldn't miss hearing.

Madden clenched his teeth as she passed his place of concealment. She was young, maybe twenty-five at most. She was beautiful. She was black.

167

For Christ's sake! Did she think her color would help her in this jungle world? The predators weren't all one color, and even if they were, they'd recognize no kinship based on skin pigment—not here. These were the rapists of social workers, the burglars of neighborhood churches, the murderers of those who—age, sex, race, and social background identical—happened to be members of rival gangs.

For God's sake! He had to stop her!

And then he realized that he couldn't. If he tried to approach her now, here, she would think that he—

When she screamed the cops would come. And it wouldn't take them long to find the pistol he carried. The pistol which had put four people in the morgue.

He couldn't try to stop her, but he could follow. Maybe, if he was quiet enough and fast enough, he could prevent what, deep down in his gut, he knew was about to happen. He could and would do his best.

He pulled the pistol from his pocket, edging back the hammer with his plastic covered thumb. Then he moved out cautiously, quietly keeping off the surfaced pathway and covering the ground as fast as he could.

Which wasn't as fast as he would have liked. The girl, obviously nervous, was moving at a fast clip, her loud heels indicating no regard for the fact that the sounds carried like cannon shots in the otherwise quiet night. Maybe that was her strategy—to signal whoever might be out there, if anybody was, that she wasn't at all afraid of them. To scare them off. Madden grimaced. Well, they are out there, lady, and they don't scare off, not through the sounds of a woman's clicking heels!

His weapon was straight up in front of him, in a military readiness carry that he thought he'd long forgotten. She was fifteen yards ahead of him now, and he was los-ing ground to her slowly but surely. By the time they got deeper into the park . . .

He decided to gamble. Not far ahead of her now was where the path crossed the East Drive. If he went straight, leaving the pathway to his right, he could dead run it and maybe cross the roadway before she did. If he could do that . . .

Enough thinking. He moved swiftly now, beginning a full run once he had plenty of trees between himself and the girl. But as he reached the road, he stopped dead. He hadn't moved fast enough. He cursed to himself again as he stood there like a statue, allowing her to cross the East Drive and once more get in front of him.

Maybe, though, she would be lucky. She already was a third of the way through. If . . .

But it was a long stretch now to the West Drive. That's where they'd be waiting.

Again he moved, again disregarding the pathway, and after crossing the road as silently as he could, breaking into an almost full run. When he drew parallel to the nearest edge of the New Lake, he stopped and listened.

He heard nothing.

*Nothing!*

# FIFTEEN

Mary Gaylord had known better, of course. But she was in a hurry. The last thing Alex Brent had told her this afternoon when he telephoned was, "Now don't you dare be late." She wasn't used to hopping when a man issued an order, but Alex Brent's order—delivered in the most humorous of tones—was something else again. That was because she wanted nothing more than to receive orders issued by Alex Brent for the rest of their natural lives.

Alex Brent, Ph.D. Columbia. Cultural anthropology was his trade and tonight he was lecturing at a special meeting at the Museum of Natural History. She'd have liked nothing more than to hear his lecture, but she'd had studying of her own to do. Economics, in which she was striving for her master's. She should have known better about that, too. She'd spent all the time she should have spent at the books trying on dress after dress and discarding each as not suitable. Alex Brent, of course, had recognized that her study time was valuable, but she could picture his face over the phone, his eyes bugging out from his black face in mock horror as he told her, "You be late, girl, and I got problems. All my audience takes off at ten, and there I'll be. In that place with all them skeleton bones!"

She'd left her apartment in what had seemed plenty of time, except she hadn't figured on the cabs. There weren't any. None with the vacant sign lighted anyway. She waited pouting on the corner of Eighty-first and Fifth for ten full minutes, at the end of which she was beginning to think that the Devil himself was conspiring to lose her her man. Then, furious, she crossed to the park side of Fifth and walked south, still hoping for a cab before she had to make the big decision.

The park. Short and direct, and plenty of time before ten. Still . . .

What made up her mind was the man. She was mid-block between Eightieth and Seventy-ninth when she saw him—going into the Seventy-ninth entrance of the park. He was wearing a light raincoat, and seemed well-dressed and well groomed. If he was going through . . .

She quickened her step. There was safety in numbers, at least there was supposed to be. If she could walk through the park close behind another person, especially a man who looked as if he might be able to take care of himself in case of trouble, whoever might otherwise think her to be easy pickings might have another thought about trying.

But when her almost running gait brought her inside the confines of the park, she couldn't see the man up ahead. He, too, probably was walking fast. She didn't blame him at all, not at all. She walked as fast as she could, cursing the uncomfortable but fashionable shoes which were made for anything but walking fast, but she tried, hoping to catch up to the very man she could not know was himself cursing her for moving as fast as she was.

She hurried across the East Drive, then almost

171

jumped at the sudden sight of Cleopatra's Needle looking up to her right.

Calm, calm, she told herself. You're almost halfway through. It wasn't true and she knew it, thus the lie didn't help much at all. *Where the hell was that man?*

If he was up ahead of her—he had to be—she'd see him soon. Just ahead and to the left would soon be the New Lake. There, for a long stretch, the pathway was almost as straight as an arrow. She might not be able to catch up with him, but just seeing him would be reassuring enough to—

It happened then. The first indication of its happening was her sudden difficulty in breathing. It took two of her now rapid heartbeats to realize that the cause of her breathing problem was a human hand—a hand which had snaked around her from behind, a hand which held her mouth closed tight, a hand which was now joined by its mate, this other hand around her waist, half lifting, half dragging her off to the right of the pathway.

Inside, she was screaming her lungs out, but nothing could break through that fierce clamp over her mouth. And then the voice.

"Don't struggle, doll—or you're dead."

There was a sudden *click* as she saw there was another of them, this one brandishing a long thin knife. *How small he looks!* But that first thought was canceled when the point of the knife touched the surface of the fur coat directly over her left breast.

"You listen good, miss," the one with the knife hissed. Then to the unseen one who still was dragging her backward: "Where you taking her, man?"

A hushed answer: "Back into the thick trees. Keep outa my way, dammit!"

*Oh God, they're going to kill me!*

And then she was pulled down to the ground. The hand still was clasped firmly around her mouth. "Bandana," the one behind her said, and now she saw a third member of the assault group, another young small black. He too had a knife in his hand, but with the other he was pulling from his pocket a large red and white bandana. He handed it over her head. And then she found out what the bandana was for.

"No sound," came the warning from behind her as the hand whipped from her mouth. Even before she could inhale deeply the bandana was in its place. Tight in place, so tight that the front of it was cutting the edges of her mouth and the knot which was tied behind was digging painfully into the place where her head met her neck.

A quick tug on the knot dropped her back flat to the earth. They stood over her. Her wildly shifting eyes could take them all in now. There weren't three of them as she had thought, but four. All black, all kids. She had one more surprise coming.

"Kill her now," said the one of them who was a girl. A scowling girl, no more than fifteen or sixteen! "Kill her and let's get out of here!"

"There ain't no hurry," whispered the leader, the biggest of them, the one who had grabbed her. "And keep your mouth quiet."

"I want the coat, okay?" the girl asked.

"Hell no, the coat we sell. Maybe gets us fifty or sixty bucks."

Fifty or sixty dollars. She was going to die for that much—and the coat had cost two hundred thirty . . .

"The purse then—I get the purse!"

The big boy nodded. "Yeah, maybe—after we see what all is in it, okay."

"Hey, Eddie, I think we should just cut her and take off—"

"With the coat and purse—and that ring," the amendment the girl put on to the smallest of the knife-carrier's suggestion.

But Eddie, obviously the tall one, shook his head slowly, smiling down at their captive. "You a nice looking chick, you know? Real rich looking stuff. I never had me a piece of rich looking stuff before."

There was another *click*. The girl now held a knife of her own and it was coming in dangerously close to Mary Gaylord's face. Behind the knife was an expression of fury.

"You want a piece of her? How about an ear—that one!"

"Shuddup!" Eddie said, a sweep of his left arm shoving the girl to the side roughly. Then he was all smiles again, for Mary. "You know what we're gonna do now, doll? You—and all of us?"

Mary squirmed, as the girl with the knife again stepped closer. "Me too?" she said with a malicious laugh.

"If you like, chile—but you last!"

Everybody thought that was funny, everybody but Mary—and somebody else. Suddenly the laughing stopped.

*"Get away from her."*

The voice wasn't loud, but it had the weight of lead. Its effect was to turn all eyes toward him, including Mary's. She knew him by the raincoat.

It was the man she had been trying to catch.

He had moved swiftly. Realizing that the lack of sound meant the girl's passage through the park had been interrupted—and realizing that interruption could mean only one thing—he ran back the way he had come, his trigger finger ready to blast at anything that moved which wasn't a black girl dressed in a fur coat. It had been their voices, hushed but loud enough, which had brought him to them. He had fully expected to find the girl nothing more than a corpse. He was relieved to find one of them talking to her.

He enjoyed their startled turns and the looks of fear which crossed their faces. He also enjoyed the sudden change of expressions—from fear to wily craftiness—as they looked at him and then at the knives they carried. His own weapon was now in his trenchcoat pocket.

"Get the mother!" one of them said. The tone of voice was deadly but it was also something else, and that something else caused Madden two seconds which might have been vital. The speaker was—a girl!

They were almost on him when his gun cleared his pocket. Much too close. His first shot caught the biggest one square in the throat, his second was taken by the center chest of another, but not before that one collided into Madden, his knife hand missing Madden's face but his forearm slamming into the stitches in his cheek. Madden felt the sharp pain as they pulled, felt the warm passage of blood.

Of the two animals left, the female had turned to run. His third shot caught her in the back of the head and she dropped in a clumsy half-cartwheel. Tiger, tigress—what was the difference? They all were of the jungle, they all used their claws.

And now to the last of them—

Who stood there, his hands above his head. Hands above his head and grinning.

"Okay, man. You from the Two Two, right?"

Madden at first didn't understand, then he remembered that there was a police precinct station in the park at about Eighty-sixth. The Twenty-second Precinct.

The kid still was talking:

"Okay. I ain't giving you no trouble, no trouble at all. That black girl there will have to testify to that. I know my rights, Mr. Policeman. You got to take me in, but before I say anything more you got to tell me my lawful rights."

The grin widened as Madden walked forward. Reaching down he took one of the switchblades and cut the kerchief from the girl's face. He pulled her to her feet.

"Thank—"

"Forget it," Madden said. "And I mean it—forget it. All of it."

Then he turned to the grinning kid.

"I have to make this quick," he said.

"Quick or slow, fuzz, you got to tell me my rights."

Madden nodded. "Okay. You've got the right to remain silent."

Then Madden put a bullet right between the kid's eyes.

Mary Gaylord waited alone with the dead a full minute before she began screaming her head off.

# *SIXTEEN*

"Jesus, Joe! I didn't know *you* got messed up—"

Hal Crosby shut his open mouth. Madden knew what the rest of it was going to be. *Too.* Just one word, but Hal couldn't say it. He let him off the hook.

"I'm afraid so, Hal." He grasped the hand which now was dangling uneasily before his co-worker. "Let's not talk about it, okay?"

Hal looked more than relieved. "Okay, Joe." But he couldn't take his eyes off the left side of Madden's face. It had had the same effect on Mrs. Greene, the vampire receptionist who for a moment forgot what drawer his second key was in. Also Jill, his secretary, had been startled by it. He had smiled at her. "You'll get used to it," he'd said.

It did look ugly. Uglier than hell. The tearing loose of the mending job last night was far from complete, but it had made his face look much less pretty than it had been. There hadn't been much blood, not as much as he'd imagined, so he'd let it go. He'd see a doctor today or tomorrow and get done what could be done.

Hal ushered him right into Chilton's office, then left, uneasily mumbling that he'd see Madden later.

Chilton stood and firmly shook Madden's hand. His eyes too focused on Madden's face, but neither they nor

177

his expression indicated that he was looking at anything unusual. He said nothing about it.

"Joe—I'm glad you're here. Sit down. Coffee?"

"No thanks." And now Madden felt uncomfortable as he sat, his eyes looking toward the door Hal had closed behind him.

Chilton sat on the edge of his desk facing Madden. "It'll pass, Joe—with them, I mean."

"Them?"

Chilton nodded. "Them. Hal and the others, your friends here. Believe me, it's more awkward for them this morning than it is for you. Think about it. Their friend and co-worker has lost his wife in horrible circumstances. Our sophisticated urban society hasn't yet developed the appropriate rituals for expressing the recognition of such a loss. Therefore everyone is ill at ease. Think about it—objectively—and I think you'll agree that I'm right."

Madden didn't much want to think about it, but he didn't want to argue. He simply nodded back to his employer. Then, because he was expected to say something, he did:

"How long?"

Chilton shrugged. "The unease? A week, two maybe, or maybe longer. It all depends on them, on you. I think, though, there's a way to shorten the time considerably. I also think that the way I have in mind would do you some good. I have no doubt that it would be to the firm's advantage." He paused, then: "Los Angeles."

Madden repeated the name of the city, not comprehending.

Chilton sighed. "The brothers Grossman. You remember them, I think."

"Some things you don't forget," Madden said.

Chilton started to laugh, then thought better of it, then laughed anyway. "Well, it's like this. Hal is against it, but I think we've got to do something to help out our favorite printing firm. It's got to be on-site, which means—"

"Which means you want me to go to L.A."

"As soon as you can. First, though—" he looked at Madden's face.

"The stitches are due out today or tomorrow. If you can recommend a good doctor—"

Chilton not only did, he had the man's office on the telephone within two minutes. An appointment was set up for the following afternoon. When the connection was broken, he smiled at Madden.

"Shall I have Sally book your flight for Wednesday morning?"

Madden sat on the edge of his bed and looked at the face of his new watch. It was a cheap, silver colored thing. He didn't want one that would remind him of the last timepiece he'd owned. Eight-thirty, the hands said. Eight-thirty—in New York.

L.A.

Chilton. The old man had Madden's interests at heart. A change of scene was supposed to do a mourning man good. Then, too, the job there was probably right. If anything could take a man's mind off himself, it was the brothers Grossman, their personalities and their problems. Also the old man probably was right about the beneficial effect of his absence upon the others in the office. Joe Madden would be back. His memos and cables would be coming in, a part of the office routine. When he returned, it would be a return from an ordi-

179

nary business trip, nothing more. It would be like any of them returning from a trip. How'd it go? How'd it *really* go? And how were the broads out there?

No, they probably wouldn't ask Joe Madden about the broads—not this time, anyway.

L.A. Los Angeles. The city of the angels. Except that it wasn't. The city was as nasty as the job he'd find waiting for him there, a city just as dirty and as much of the jungle as New York. And, that being the case . . .

He was mildly surprised to find that he was fondling the .38. As he looked up from it, his eyes found his reflection in the mirror facing the bed. He was not surprised at the smile his reflection returned to him.

He stood and reached for his trenchcoat, the revolver still in his hand.

He was going to the opposite side of the continent on Wednesday. That left him two more nights in Manhattan.

He was determined to put them to good use.

PINNACLE BOOKS

# THE INCREDIBLE ACTION PACKED SERIES

# DEATH MERCHANT

## by Joseph Rosenberger

His name is Richard Camellion, he's a master of disguise, deception and destruction. He does what the CIA and FBI cannot do. They call him THE DEATH MERCHANT!

| Order | | Title | Book # | Price |
|---|---|---|---|---|
| _____ | # 1 | THE DEATH MERCHANT | P211 | .95¢ |
| _____ | # 2 | OPERATION OVERKILL | P245 | .95¢ |
| _____ | # 3 | THE PSYCHOTRON PLOT | P117 | .95¢ |
| _____ | # 4 | CHINESE CONSPIRACY | P168 | .95¢ |
| _____ | # 5 | SATAN STRIKE | P182 | .95¢ |
| _____ | # 6 | ALBANIAN CONNECTION | P670 | $1.25 |
| _____ | # 7 | CASTRO FILE | P264 | .95¢ |
| _____ | # 8 | BILLIONAIRE MISSION | P339 | .95¢ |
| _____ | # 9 | THE LASER WAR | P399 | .95¢ |
| _____ | #10 | THE MAINLINE PLOT | P473 | $1.25 |
| _____ | #11 | MANHATTAN WIPEOUT | P561 | $1.25 |
| _____ | #12 | THE KGB FRAME | P642 | $1.25 |
| _____ | #13 | THE MATO GROSSO HORROR | P705 | $1.25 |

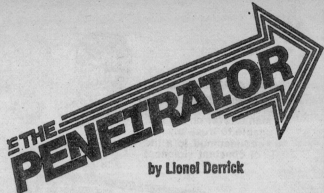

# THE PENETRATOR

### by Lionel Derrick

Mark Hardin. Discharged from the army, after service in Vietnam. His military career was over. But *his* war was just beginning. His reason for living and reason for dying become the same—to stamp out crime and corruption wherever he finds it. He is deadly; he is unpredictable; and he is dedicated. He is The Penetrator!

Read all of him in: